CUPID'S FAVOR

NAUGHTY CUPID SERIES ANNIVERSARY EDITION

MICHELLE M. PILLOW

MICHELLEPILLOW.COM

Cupid's Favor
Paranormal Fantasy Romance
Naughty Cupid Book Three

Beware of trolls bearing favors.

When Lord Malak saves Cupid from a sandpit, the troll is honor bound to settle the life debt or risk being called upon later—even if the lycan noble insists he doesn't want any reward for the deed. Simply breeding the man's goats isn't enough to repay such a price. No, for this he needs something more. Knowing the perfect gift to be revenge, Cupid delivers the one thing that seems to aggravate Lord Malak the most—Lady Sophia.

After being kidnapped and drugged by the horrible Cupid, Lady Sophia wants to go home—to a place where magic doesn't exist and there's no chance of being eaten by a dragon. But most of all, she wants to be rid of her escort, Lord Malak. The charming lycan swore to protect her and see her safely home, but it seems fate and a little troll have other plans.

Author recommends reading books in order of release. For details please visit www.michellepillow.com

*To those who don't like Valentine's Day—a Cupid even
you can love.*

Cupid's Enchantment
Cupid's Revenge
Cupid's Favor

The Playful Prince
The Bound Prince
The Rogue Prince
The Pirate Prince

Qurilixen Lords
Dragon Prince
More Coming Soon!

Captured by a Dragon-Shifter Series
Determined Prince
Rebellious Prince
Stranded with the Cajun
Hunted by the Dragon
Mischievous Prince
Headstrong Prince

Space Lords Series
His Frost Maiden
His Fire Maiden

His Metal Maiden

His Earth Maiden

His Woodland Maiden - Coming Soon

Dynasty Lords Series

Seduction of the Phoenix

Temptation of the Butterfly

Having trouble finding the books?

Updated Buy Links Here

To learn more about the Qurilixen World series of books
and to stay up to date on the latest book list visit
www.MichellePillow.com

PROLOGUE

Cupid brushed sand off his arms, mumbling to himself. He frowned, not liking what he had to do, but a debt was a debt. His beady, black eyes flashed with an inner fire. He might be many things, but a troll who reneged on a life debt was not one of them.

Lord Malak had pulled him from the quicksand and saved his life. Now Cupid owed him a great favor in return, even if the lycan noble insisted he didn't want it. If Cupid didn't give it to him now, he knew that someday Malak could come back to call upon him, and that was something he refused to accept. It was bad enough he would be forced to help a lycan, but to be in Malak's debt? No, that would be worse.

So, what to do? No small feat would repay a life debt.

He couldn't merely breed Malak's goats for this one. He needed something big. He needed something grand.

Love?

Cupid nearly gagged as the thought popped into his head. He hit himself on the ear to get it out. A gooey clump of sand fell out instead. Love? Why in all the realms would he think of love? He hated love. He hated the way people looked while they were in it. The way they talked, acted, swooned, and kissed.

Bah. Ach.

Cupid hacked, spitting sand on the ground. The grains were everywhere, rubbing into every crease, chaffing his flesh. Worst of all, the sinkhole had cleaned him of his most glorious stench. He hadn't bathed in decades. It would take him forever to get that smell back.

Damn King Larus for throwing him into the sinkhole and Lord Ilar for letting him. So what if the two were bitter about what he'd done to them? The trolls still teased him about helping Lord Ilar and Lady Rhiannon fall in love, and now he'd be ridiculed for King Larus and Lady Mina as well. Could he allow another blemish to surface on his name?

Bah. No.

No, love was no way to repay a debt to the lycan who saved his life. Ah, but hate. Now there was a real idea. Hate was much better than love. Hate made your blood boil and your heart race. It made you feel alive and gave you purpose. Aye, hate. He'd have to watch Lord Malak very closely and figure out whom he hated the most. Then, Cupid would bring that creature before Lord Malak to destroy.

Hate. Cupid rubbed his gnarled, wrinkled hands together. A smile spread over his flat, wide lips. Now this was a good idea. Besides, what better way to squelch his undeserved reputation as a matchmaker than to help a lycan find his revenge?

LYCAON CASTLE, REALM OF MAGIC, 1407 AD

"Lady Sophia."

Lady Sophia of Aucester looked at the guard, feeling nauseous. He was very tan with dark hair and eyes and was smaller in build than some of his brethren. His words were a low growl as he said her name, causing her to shiver in revulsion. All the lycans' words were a low growl. It was as if they were all on the brink of attacking.

But it wasn't only the way the lycans talked that bothered her. They dressed indecently in draping tunics that fell to the tops of their knees. Like the guard before her in the large square piece of brown material that wrapped his waist and was held over one shoulder with a brooch, leaving his muscular calves, arms and a shoulder bare. On his feet was a pair of short boots with leather cross lacing winding up his legs. Even the lycan women wore a floor length version of the garb. There was no mistaking the fact that they could part from their clothing at a moment's notice and stand naked for all to see.

Even though the man looked human, Sophia knew he wasn't. He was a lycan, a man-beast, a *nieten*. It didn't matter what word she used to describe them; they all meant the same thing—men who shifted into horrible, unholy wolves. They were magical creatures in a magical realm. She hated them, hated the realm of immortals and magic. She wanted to go home to her human world, where men stayed men and animals were hunted for food.

Sophia couldn't help being bitter. A horrible little troll named Cupid had kidnapped her and her sister, Mina, and brought them to the realm of all things magical. At first glance this realm wasn't so different from the human world, from her home in Wessex. The landscape was the same, though the sky was a little too purple and the trees were a little too red.

Sophia looked around Lycaon Castle's inner courtyard. The castle was not like her dilapidated home. Lycaon was a grand palace, opulent and fine. The battlements circled the bailey, disappearing in the distance. Square turrets were built in intervals along the outer face, standing tall as lookout towers. A stone house encased the gated entrance. The gate was up so people could walk through it freely. If she were in her world, she would have killed for a chance to live in such a place. It wasn't as if she had a lot to go back to. Since her father had been murdered for going against his king, she and her sister had been left in ruin, without family, money-less, friendless, and most likely soon to be homeless once King Henry granted their lands to a nobleman he felt worthy of lording over it.

The lycan palace might look undaunting in design, but the people of this realm were another matter alto-gether. The lycans were beasts. Their castle might be nice, but it couldn't hide the primitives dwelling within the walls. Every time she saw one of them she shook with fright and if they came too close, she had to suppress tears of desperation and outrage at what had been done to her.

"Tal," Lady Rhiannon acknowledged the guard when Sophia did not. She blinked, realizing the beast man still stood before her, staring as if he would like nothing more than to devour her whole.

Their hostess, Lady Rhiannon, was human. She'd been enchanted by Cupid and brought to the magic realm before Sophia and Mina's kidnapping. Rhiannon's enchantment was said to have brought all the lycan men howling to their knees in desire for her. Lucky, or unluckily to Sophia's thinking, Rhiannon had fallen in love with the very lycan she was meant to punish. Lord Ilar, Commander of the Lycan Guard, had mated to Rhiannon and they were now living happily ever after. Once mated, the other wolves let her be.

Sophia glanced over at the woman. Rhiannon was beautiful, with long curly blonde hair and blue-gray eyes. She looked so... normal. Sophia didn't know why the woman chose to stay in this world.

Next to Rhiannon was Sophia's sister. Mina had been brought to the realm the same time Sophia was. Cupid, seeking to avenge himself against the lycan king, had kidnapped them. It was a fact Sophia was still bitter about. When Cupid took Rhiannon, he enchanted the lycans to pursue her. When he took Sophia and her sister, Cupid did the opposite. He struck Larus with a magical love dart and Sophia had fallen hopelessly in love with the king. Mina had been unaffected by the whole affair—unless you counted the fact that she'd had sex with the lycan king and was now lovesick over him the old-fashioned, natural way.

Sophia wished she would have been as lucky as the other two as to have kept her wits about her. But, no. She'd been utterly in love with King Larus, mindless and blind to anything else, until every breath she took was for him. Then, to make matters worse, she was kidnapped by a vampire named Devlin and had fallen in love with him as well, mesmerized by his powerful, magical eyes to do so.

Sophia shivered. Twice she'd been in love, neither time her will or her doing. After the enchantment ended, she was left heartbroken with all the pain but no one to mourn or fight for, no one who returned the feelings she had harbored so dear. She swore that there would never be a third time. No man would ever touch her heart again. She didn't think she could survive it.

All three human women were seated on a bench trying to enjoy the afternoon weather—that was until the lycan guard tried to talk to them. All simple pleasures in the day had fled with his presence.

Both sisters were dressed as Rhiannon, who'd adopted the look of the lycans. The undertunic, meant to protect the women's delicate human skin, was the only difference to the lycans' garb. The sleeved undertunics were much like the ones they wore back home, but the long rectangle of the overdress was like the female lycans. It loosely wound around the body, pinning at the shoulder. Though Sophia would never admit to it, the gown was comfortable.

Sighing, Sophia turned to look at her sister. Mina could well have been her twin, though she was a few years older and had locks as black as night instead of her golden waves. Their faces were nearly identical, down to their light brown eyes and the shape of their noses. They were the same height and the same slender build and even shared the same fullness of lips that had garnered the interest of many men. The men who'd wanted to marry them before their father had been executed by King Henry now wanted the sisters to be their whores.

Sophia frowned. Was she a fool to long for the human world? It wasn't like it had been kind to her. Lycan or mortal, all men were the same. Rutting pigs. The only reason she preferred mortals was they didn't possess the added threat of magic and fangs.

"We would like to tournament to be Lady Sophia's lover," Tal stated, bringing her attention back to him. Sophia gagged, unable to help the natural reflex. Mina instantly put a protective hand on her arm. Rhiannon's smile faded.

"No," Sophia croaked, pushing to her feet. The sooner she left Lycaon the better.

"But...?" Tal looked confused. His eyes bore into her and Sophia couldn't meet them, didn't want to. He looked at her like all the man-beasts looked at her—like she was a piece of meat ready to be torn apart. Rhiannon had said she could have her pick from any of them for a mate or a lover. But Sophia didn't want the lycan men, didn't want any man. Tal continued to speak, not taking his greedy eyes off her, "She said she wished to judge for the position. It has been decided. Only those with good teeth will compete."

Sophia stiffened. They had heard that? She'd been joking, bitterly spouting off at the mouth to shock Mina who had slept with the lycan king. Mina was enamored with King Larus. Any fool could see it well enough. The idea that her sister had fornicated with the man made her sick.

Sophia saw the man eyeing her and tried to remember what exactly she'd said. She was pretty sure it had something to do with choosing a lover like she would a good stallion—good teeth, decent bloodline, a fine gait and superior form. Someone wild and strong, but also someone she could bend to her will. Then, when she controlled them, she would get herself a new one.

It might have been a joke, but the idea had merit. Men used their bodies all the time in battle and for what? Fortune? Glory? Power? Why should she not use her body to survive? At least then it would be on her own terms. Only, it wouldn't be with a lycan, but a human. None of these man-beasts were going to touch her.

"Come Sophia, let's go," Mina said.

Sophia nodded in agreement. As they walked away,

Sophia heard Tal say, "Did she not say she wished to pick one out?"

"It is, ah, flattering they wish to tournament for you," Mina said when they were alone.

"To be their whore." Sophia walked toward the stairs that led their shared room. She was fed up with it all, tired of being wanted for her body. Mina moved to follow her. Sophia stopped and held up her hand. She needed time alone to collect herself. "No, Mina, let me be alone for a moment."

The large fireplace burned brightly, casting the gray bedchamber walls with a golden light. King Larus had given Sophia and Mina the guest bedchamber upon arriving at Lycaon. The room was spacious, doubling as a bower. Beautifully carved high-backed chairs with plush cushioned seats were near a long-slotted window. Next to the chairs was a carved table of dark wood. Strange rugs were beneath the window, made from a type of wool.

Sophia crossed over to look out the window. It was a beautiful room, one she would be happy in on any other occasion. The only thing waiting for her back home was a burnt out, empty keep. No one worried for her or cared. The only person she had was her sister.

Sophia heard the door open. She took a deep breath as tension seized her but didn't move otherwise. By the sound of the footfall she could tell it was Mina and forced her body to relax.

"I want to stay," Mina said. Sophia stiffened at the words. "I've thought about it and I think we should stay here."

"Mina," Sophia began, turning to look at her. Slowly, she shook her head in denial. She couldn't speak. How could she make her sister understand? The only way a human could survive in this world was to have a man-beast's protection. She would be beholden to no man unless it were on her own terms. Back home, she could protect herself. The sisters had survived two years on their own, abandoned and starving. They could continue to do so.

"There's nothing left for us in our world," Mina insisted. "Larus has put us under his protection. It's more than we could hope for—"

"You don't mean that." Inside Sophia shook violently, near tears. On the outside, she remained calm. She wouldn't stay only to have Mina reduced to being a king's whore. It was clear Mina was smitten, but that was no reason to remain. Sophia wasn't a fool. She knew her sister thought to be in love with the lycan king. But, how would they ever know if the love was true? She herself thought to be in love with the very same man. She would have laid down her life for him. But it had been a spell that made her feel such strong emotions. "How could we possibly stay here? Why?"

"Adventure," Mina answered, not meeting her eyes. "You wanted to see the world, well here we are. This is more world than you'll ever find back home. Let's stay. We have nothing to go back to, no one. We can adjust to the magic, the creatures. They said that humans tried to harness magic in the past which means we can use magic to get us by. We can learn."

"I have no wish to stay in this place, Mina."

"You won't even consider it?" Mina rested a hand on her shoulder. Sophia shrugged it off. "For a short time at least? See if it agrees with us once we know more?"

"You can't know what it's like to be violated as I have been," Sophia said. How could she explain that she couldn't risk being mesmerized by a vampire or doused with a magic that took away her will? At least in the human world the odds will be fair. No enchantments, no mysteriously swirling eyes. "You haven't been through what I've been through."

Mina was quiet.

When it became apparent her sister wasn't going to

answer, Sophia continued, "You've found something, someone. I've got nothing here, but you. That vampire drank from my neck, Mina. He drank my blood and I let him, was *happy* to let him. He looked into my eyes and I would have let him do anything he wanted to me. He could have said to hold still while he cut off my limbs one by one and I would have let him."

"Did Lord Devlin hurt you?" Mina asked. "Did he...?"

"No, my maidenhead is intact." Sophia swiped angrily at her eyes as they filled with tears. "But he could have is my point. I don't want to be here. I don't want there to be a next time. I had no will, no fight in me. And I loved Devlin. When he looked at me, I loved him more than myself. And when I saw Larus, every breath I took was for him. I felt love Mina, as true as I'm ever likely to find it, truer than I ever want to feel it again. But it wasn't real. I don't love Larus or Devlin, but the feelings I had for them were so real. It's like my heart has been ripped out, only there was no one to rip it, no one to mourn. I don't have a name or a face. I don't have someone to fight for. All I have is the emptiness left behind now that the love is gone. I never want my happiness, my very sanity, to be dependent on another's feelings for me. I don't wish to be that helpless."

Sophia shivered as Mina hugged her tightly to her chest. "I won't let anything happen to you. I promise."

"I would rather they'd raped my body instead of my mind," Sophia whispered. "I had no control over myself and I almost killed you because of it. I never want to feel out of control again. I have to leave this world. Don't you understand, Mina? I can't stay."

Mina nodded slowly. Sophia felt a strange sense of relief. If she could get home, the ache inside her heart would end.

"You're right, Sophia," Mina agreed. "You can't. I won't either. I can't let you go back alone. I won't abandon you. You are my blood."

Lord Malak smiled as he walked into Lycaon's main hall to greet his old friends—King Larus and Commander Ilar. It wasn't solely friendship that brought him to Lycaon, but the summons he had received from King Larus. Malak's smile widened. According to the messenger, two unclaimed human females were running around Larus's castle causing havoc on the unmated males.

Malak had to admit he was very curious about the situation. It seemed like mortal women were popping up everywhere. First Lady Rhiannon was brought to Lycaon, ultimately mating his friend Ilar, and now there were two more humans. Rumor had it that the lycan king had marked one of the women for himself. Though Larus hadn't technically mated to her yet, he had taken her as a lover.

How strange it was to have humans turning up now, after so long. Mortals and immortals had fought long ago. It had been a horrible war, one with much death on both sides. In the end, it was decided the realms should be forever separated. That was why the portals had been sealed. That is why many believed they must remain sealed. Malak didn't have an opinion on the matter. He'd learned that time changes everything and to take all life had to offer in stride. Immortality was too long a time to stick to a conviction, so he tended to make very little of them.

Only a few natural portals remained between the two magic and mortal worlds, as they couldn't be destroyed. His land was home to one of them and it had been his duty to guard it. The portal doors on the mortal side were locked with strong charms. The only way the portals could be opened was from the immortal's side. But, once opened, the realms could merge freely.

Mm, Malak thought, licking his lips. It had been a long time since he'd slept with a human woman. If he remembered, they had incredibly soft bodies and made the cutest little noises in bed. Just thinking of sex made his shaft stir beneath his tunic. Malak suppressed a groan. He was well used to his heightened sexual appetites and chose to ignore his desire for the moment.

Seeing Ilar and Larus, Malak went to the raised dining platform. A fire burned brightly over the hall. Fairies danced about in a corner. The pretty little things were very vain and no bigger than butterflies. Lower tables lined a good part of the stone floor and he had to step around them. Some of the guards were gathered, drinking and talking amongst themselves in leisure. A few of the lycan women joined the men and Malak automatically smiled at the females, unable to help himself as they gave him provocative looks.

"Malak," Larus greeted him, using the old human language. Malak took it in stride. Since Lady Rhiannon's arrival, those at Lycaon had slipped into the human language so she would be more comfortable. "Thank you for coming."

Malak nodded, noticing the lines of stress on the king's face. He answered in the old language, saying, "I hear there are more mortal women running about your keep."

Malak went to the head table and picked up Ilar's wine goblet to take a sip. Seeing a maid staring at him in open invitation, he grinned. Tipping the rim at her in acknowledgment, he then drank the king's wine and placed the empty goblet on the table. Ilar gave him a bemused look but said nothing.

"Ah, how could I stay away from such news?" Malak kept his smile. "Tell me, Larus, how is it Lycaon gets all the new females and Fenris is overrun with the same ones? I have half a mind to find Cupid and insult him myself if it will bring pretty women to my door."

Larus merely grunted, saying nothing.

It was no secret that Cupid was behind all three mortal women being in the magic realm. In fact, Malak had seen Cupid on his way to the castle. The troll's hands had been sticking out of quicksand and Malak saved the creature before he realized who it was. If he hadn't, he was sure Cupid would have made his way of the pit eventually, but the troll was begrudgingly grateful for the rescue.

When the king didn't respond to his jest, Malak glanced at Ilar in question. The commander shook his head slightly, not giving an answer. Now this was more interesting than Malak first thought. Could it be that Larus wanted more from his human lover than bodily pleasures? Malak wasn't one for commitment, but he would gladly welcome his friend to it.

"Your man was very vague in the details, my king," Malak said, leaning against the table. He drew his finger lazily over the top, gauging Larus's reaction. The maid that he'd tipped the goblet to came forward with a drink for him and he took it, smiling charmingly at her. When she left, he continued, "All he would tell me is that there were two mortal women, and you wished me to take them to Fenris with me."

"To the portals," Larus corrected him. "It's my wish that you see them safely back to their home."

"Ah," Malak frowned. That mission didn't sound quite as fun. Still watching the king for a reaction, and mischievously tempted to provoke his old friend, he said lightly, "I had hoped that you wished me to mate with them. From your man's descriptions, I've had fantasies aplenty of two beautiful sisters."

"You are a pig."

Malak looked around in surprise. It took him a moment to register that the contrary tone was directed at him. Women never yelled at him, unless it was to scream out his name with pleasure.

Or while throwing things at my back because I refuse to give them pleasure, Malak thought, doing his best to suppress an arrogant grin. So what if it was a little conceited? It was also true.

As he met brown eyes spitting fire in his direction, Malak froze. Instantly he knew her for a mortal by her smell. She wore the dress of his kind, but with the added protection of an undertunic. It was too bad. Malak would have liked to see the curve of her neck more clearly, as it led to the delectable bend of her shoulders and arms, perhaps with a tempting peek of her rounded breasts along the sides.

His usual state of arousal intensified, unfurling in his blood. She was a slender thing—almost too slender from the look of her frame. Long waves of blonde silk spilled over her shoulders, just as soft and tempting as her flesh would be. How he wanted to bury his face in her hair as he buried his rod inside her hot, moist body.

Instantly, the rogue in him surfaced, ready to seduce. He pushed up from where he leaned against the table and bowed to her. Lowering his tone to a seductive drawl, he said, "My lady. I can assure you I'm quite the wolf."

Instead of the simpering smile he expected, she grimaced at him. Looking down her nose as if he'd insulted her by being in her presence, she narrowed her eyes in apparent disdain. She didn't even try to hide the emotion.

"And I am quite the hunter," she spat. "I do enjoy skinning wolves. Speak of my sister or me in such a way again and I'll be more than happy to turn your ugly hide into a rug."

Malak opened his mouth, but he didn't know what to say. The woman shot him one last nasty look and stormed off. He glanced back to the head table in amazement, not sure whether to be insulted or turned on by the mortal. Larus and Ilar exchanged amused looks. No wonder they laughed. They were unloading the disagreeable wench on him.

"By all the lycan *that* wench is the shrew you wish for me to escort to a portal?" Malak grimaced. With his sudden, intense desire for the woman and her obvious dislike of him it would be an arduous journey. "I can see why you don't wish to go yourself. Pray, let me kick her through it with the bottom of my boot."

"That is Lady Sophia," Ilar said, looking at the stairwell where the woman had disappeared.

"She is under my protection, Malak," Larus added, his tone stern.

Since Larus's eyes hadn't lit with possession and he could smell no mark on the blonde-haired vixen, Malak already assumed that she wasn't the king's mistress. With Sophia's temperament, Malak did have to admit that the challenge she presented was stirring to his primitive nature. The beast in him wanted to tame and subdue her. The man in him wanted to do much more than that.

"I'd have your pledge to guard her and her sister with your life," Larus continued, drawing Malak from thoughts of holding the stubborn woman down and devouring every supple inch of her body. "I'll entrust them into your care from the moment you leave until they are safely through the portal."

"If you ask it, it is done," Malak said without hesitation. He meant it, too, as he placed a fist over his heart. "I give you my word of honor."

The king nodded. Malak again turned to look at the stairwell. "It's true that Cupid brought the two sisters here, enchanting them?"

Larus sighed. "Actually, he shot me with the dart while I was in the forest. Though Lady Mina was unaffected by it, Lady Sophia was the victim of its effects. I think it's best if you leave her alone about it. She's very..."

"Shrewish?" Malak supplied. "Difficult?"

"It is fun when they resist you, isn't it?" Ilar said, more to himself. Malak grinned.

"I was going to say sensitive about what happened," the king put forth. "She deserves consideration."

"And this other lady? Lady Mina?" Malak asked.

Larus's face hardened and he stood. Very quietly, he whispered, "They are my wards, Malak. Treat them as such."

Larus walked away. Malak's playful expression fell as he looked at Ilar.

"He loves Mina," Ilar said. "Rhiannon believes Mina loves him as well."

"Then?" Malak asked, curious.

"I believe Mina goes because it is Sophia's wish," Ilar said.

"Sophia would deny her sister happiness?" Malak was appalled. How selfish was this Sophia?

"Nothing is ever so simple, friend," Ilar said, before changing the subject. "Now, come. Tell me of Fenris. What news have you from your decadent court?"

Malak nodded, effortlessly changing subjects, even as his eyes still strayed to the stairwell. "Debauchery, drinking, gaming, fighting, you know the usual diversions."

Sᴏᴘʜɪᴀ ᴡᴀs ʟɪᴠɪᴅ ᴀs sʜᴇ ᴍᴀᴅᴇ ʜᴇʀ ᴡᴀʏ ᴜᴘ ᴛʜᴇ stairwell to go to the room she shared with Mina. Out of all the lycans she'd met since being in the magic realm, Lord Malak was the most insufferable. He thought he was so charming, with his raven black hair flowing in waves about his muscled shoulders. The locks were so long they nearly touched his waist. Or what about those gray-green eyes of his that were all mischievous? Yeah, Sophia knew what kind of mischief he wanted to be about. She'd seen the lecherous intent in his eyes. He was like all the other lycans here, just wanting to get up her skirts.

Oh, and did he think it was proper to walk around bare-chested like he did? Sophia's heart beat a little faster and she didn't like the reaction one bit. Sure, he wore a tunic, but it was merely wrapped around his waist like he'd come from a bath. Even in this primitive castle, where the men all wore draping tunics slashed over one shoulder, surely his half-naked state was unacceptable. Okay, so a few others didn't drape their tunics to hide their chest, but it didn't make it right. Like anyone wanted to see all those bulging muscles. Or his trim waist. Or the light sprinkling of hair that covered his strong calves, leading up underneath the edge of the draping tunic to where his...

Sophia took a deep, furious breath. There was absolutely nothing appealing about the barbaric man. Pushing open the bedchamber door, she saw Mina resting on the bed. Her sister moved and Sophia knew she was awake.

"Lord Malak has arrived," Sophia said, coming into the chamber, snarling as she said his name. "He is the most insufferable toad. The nerve of him."

"I'm sure he's fine," Mina said, sniffing. Something in her voice made Sophia stop. Mina's eyes were red and swollen. She'd been crying, hard.

"Mina?" Sophia asked, going to her side. She sat on the mattress, reaching for her sister's back as Mina tried to bury her face in the mattress. "What is it?"

"Nothing." Mina's voice was muffled.

Sophia took a deep breath. How could she be so selfish? Seeing the heartbreak on her sister's face, she understood. Sophia felt that way over two men—men that didn't really exist. Mina's man was real. She thought back to the main hall. Larus's expression had been just as strained. Perhaps he did love her sister. And why wouldn't he? There was so much about Mina worth loving.

"You love him, don't you? It's not lovesickness. You really do love him," Sophia said softly, having to force the words. Mina cried harder, nodding frantically into the mattress. Sophia closed her eyes. She should never have begged Mina to go back to the mortal realm with her. Her sister's place was with her heart. "Have you told him?"

"I... I can't," Mina said. "There's no point. We're leaving forever."

"You wear your heart in your eyes, Mina," Sophia said. "I was a fool not to have seen it before now. I've felt the love you have. Only it's no spell that put yours there, is it?"

"Don't." Mina sniffed back tears. "I... I don't want to talk about it."

"My heart was broken by a troll's magic. Nothing can be done for that. But you, Mina, your heart will be broken by your actions." Sophia moved to the slit of a window to look the courtyard filled with lycans. It took all her energy not to cry out in frustration. She was happy for Mina and jealous of her at the same time. "I can't live knowing my selfishness took you from your happiness. You deserve happiness."

"I must take care of you. It's my duty as the eldest."

That broke Sophia's heart. After their father died, Mina had taken over and Sophia had let her. Mina had looked out for her their entire lives.

"No, Mina, no." Sophia turned to her, looking at the face so like her own. Only there was a way to lessen the misery in Mina's expression. "I'm too old for a caretaker. You've done your duty by me, but it is time you looked to yourself. Go to him. Tell him how you feel. If he'll have you, stay. If he won't have you, then he is a fool. Larus may seem many things to me, but a fool is not one of them."

"Sophia...? Won't you reconsider? Stay with me," Mina begged. "Stay here. You don't have to marry. You're the king's ward. You'll have food and shelter and we'll be together. You won't starve or freeze. Please, consider it."

The idea of a lonely future frightened her. Sophia knew what awaited her in the human realm. She had no other family. Their home was a crumbling shell with no servants. Everyone they loved was either dead or had abandoned them. It was highly possible she would freeze or starve when she returned. Before Cupid kidnapped them that is exactly what the sisters had been doing.

And yet, Sophia would choose that life over living in the magic realm. Physical pain could be endured. The ache magic had put in her heart could not. Their feelings were the one thing King Henry had not been able to take away from them. The human king took their home, their father, their reputation, but he could not take her spirit. No. The magic realm had done that.

There was no answer to this situation that would result in Sophia's happiness so she had to pick the option that would help her keep her sanity. To see Mina with Larus would break her heart anew each time she witnessed it. Cupid's spell made her fall in love, so completely. The lycans only reminded her of it. Then there was the vampire. Though shorter lived, that love had been just as strong. And now it was gone, taken to a place that never existed.

The feeling reminded her of the day she saw her father's body hanging—the fear, the pain, the uncertainty —only it was much worse. During the atrocities of the mortal realm, Sophia had been able to cling to her free will. No matter what was done to her, they could not control her thoughts or force her not to feel.

All she could do was give her sister a future. Mina

deserved so much. Here Mina would not starve. She'd have shelter and protection. She would have a true love.

"You know my reasons." Even now Sophia feared some creature would appear and make her a slave to their will. "I can't stay, and you can't go."

"Sop—"

"No," Sophia said, trying to hold back her emotions. "I said go to him. Now."

Mina stood from the bed and rushed to wrap her arms around her. "I love you."

"I know. Go tell it to the man who doesn't." Sophia said. When her sister didn't move fast enough, Sophia patted Mina's cheek before nudging her gently toward the door. "It's all right. I promise. Go, Mina."

When she was alone, Sophia turned back to the window. Nothing in life had turned out the way it was supposed to.

4

Sophia glanced over the crowded hall, watching her sister. Things had worked out well for Mina and Larus. She was a little surprised when they announced their marriage merely an hour after Mina left her, but seeing Mina's happy face reassured Sophia that her sister made the right decision. Larus's love was there for all to see as well. If any marriage had a good chance at making it, theirs did. Even through her hate of the magical world, she could admit that much.

The lycan's were celebrating their king's wedding with a great feast. A small group played music as others danced. Bonfires were lit outside, sending a soft glow through the door. Inside in the hall the light from the fireplace kept the room in shadows. Mead, ale, wine and a few drinks she'd never heard of were being generously poured. Everyone else was having a good time. Sophia tried to smile, tried to join in the celebration, but she couldn't. With each passing second, she felt more and more alone.

Watching as another lycan came up to where she sat alone at the head table, she scowled at him. Like all his kind, he had an abundance of muscles on his lean frame. His blond hair was tied back from his chiseled face, falling over his back. He didn't appear to mind her ill humor because he kept walking toward her. She already knew what he was going to ask before he opened his mouth. It was the same question nearly twenty before him had braved.

"My lady," the lycan guard bowed, "will you join me for a dance?"

Sophia looked at him and flatly answered, "No."

His mouth opened again as if he would speak.

"No." She didn't want to hear whatever flowery words he'd prepared to woo her.

"Bu—"

"No," Sophia repeated. She could do this all night if she had to. In fact, she had been doing it all night. She didn't want to dance. She didn't want to go for a stroll. She didn't want them to fight each other for her honor. She didn't want anything to do with the male sex.

"I," the man tried. He was persistent. She'd give him that.

"No." Her tone didn't change.

"You heard the lady, Dolan."

Sophia frowned. She'd only talked to him one time, but she recognized Lord Malak's voice without even looking.

The lycan bowed, shot her a lopsided grin and backed away. Sophia ignored him, not sorry to see him go. To her dismay, a shiver worked over her as she turned slowly to look at Malak. Treacherous body. How dare it try to feel pleasure at his attempt to rescue her?

She expected to feel repulsion, tried to feel it. Instead, a slow warmth invaded her at his devilishly charming smile. It was almost as if he couldn't help the charismatic look.

More black magic, she assured herself. First Cupid enchanted her to Larus and now Malak was doing something to make her like him. She'd felt some of these feelings before when she thought to be in love with Larus—her body pulling toward him, her heart racing a little, her lower stomach aching to be touched.

Sophia wasn't a fool. She knew what that aching meant. No man had ever touched her there, but it didn't mean she'd never touched herself. There was a lot to be learned by dressing up as a boy and sneaking around her father's castle during festivals. She never told Mina, knowing her sister would put a stop to such activities.

That was a long time ago. Sophia was no longer a child, but the lessons she'd learned and the things she saw were still embedded in her mind. She knew what Malak and all these man-beasts wanted when they eyed her like that. She'd seen the knights look at the maids the same way. They wanted to lift her skirts and have their way with her, maybe beget a bastard and leave her behind to deal with it.

No, thank you.

Sophia knew, had always known, that if she let a man cross that boundary it would be on her terms and for her pleasure. She wasn't saving herself for marriage. She was saving herself for the right moment. Malak's eyes seemed to glow. Anticipation gathered between her thighs from looking at him and she felt a little jolt of excitement. Despite what her insides seemed to want, Malak was not going to be that *right moment.*

With Larus and the vampire Devlin, these feelings had been the doing of a malicious spell. Why would the sensation she felt with Malak now be any different? Sophia wasn't going to be caught off guard again. She'd be keeping a close eye on him.

"Your eyes stare at me, my lady, flickering between

pleasure and hatred," Malak said, slipping into the chair next to her uninvited. He set a goblet down on the table and leaned toward her, his breath smelling of stout liquor. His hand skirted lightly onto her thigh. She tensed. "Tell me, which would you have me react to? The hatred or the pleasure?"

The way he said *the pleasure*, his voice rumbling low in his throat, made her tremble. She jerked her leg away, slapping his hand back at the same time. "Unhand me, brute, or I will relieve you of your hand."

"Did you threaten to cut my hand off?" Malak asked in surprise. He tipped his head back, laughing heartily. Sophia stared out over the hall, anything to keep from looking at his handsomely chiseled features.

"You did say you were from Fenris? Named after the Norse wolf Fenrir, I suppose?" Sophia asked, somewhat changing the subject. "I've heard the stories. A wild beast that bit off the hand of the one god who fed him."

"*Mm*, tell me, in this tale are you the wild beast and I the god that should try to tame you?" Malak's grin widened. He lifted his hand and offered it to her, palm up, as if daring her to try to relieve him of it. There was no fear in him, despite her heated words. Familiar calluses were on his hand. This man used a sword and often. His thigh brushed hers as he moved and she wondered if it was an accident. Seeing his expression, she somehow doubted it. "Is that an invitation, my lady?"

"No, I was thinking it fitting. You are after all primitive, beast-like, and clearly not very smart. Like a wolf stupid enough to bite the hand that gives it food. I wonder if you will run so well with a missing paw." Sophia made a move to stand. Malak grabbed her thigh, squeezing enough to make her remain seated.

Sophia's heart leapt in her chest. What was it about this man that made her all jittery inside? She again tried to move her leg away, but he only squeezed harder. This wasn't a caress, but a warning. She felt the strength in him. If he wanted, he could break her leg without expending but an ounce of energy.

Malak's pleasant expression stayed intact, but his eyes hardened, the gray-green depths swirling with hints of gold. He leaned closer to her. The smell of liquor from his breath fanned over her and she knew he could very well be drunk, though he held himself well. She felt the heat of his naked chest on her arm and was soon after accosted by the earthy, musky smell of his body. Her skin tingled in response.

"I may be a primitive beast, my lady, but you are rude and arrogant and," he glanced over her, "definitely think too highly of yourself and your charms."

"Well," Sophia returned, desperately searching for

an insult and having a hard time thinking of anything other than the fact that his hand had slid a little higher on her upper thigh. Wait a minute. Did he imply she wasn't that pretty? "You're... *drunk.*"

"You need to be," he returned easily. "Maybe then you'd realize this is a celebration and you should at least be pretending to have a good time, which brings me to my purpose in sitting by you. People are beginning to suspect that you don't approve of your sister's good fortune in marrying our king. You sit here, snarling at every man who asks you to dance as if they're going to ravish you right here in the hall. In fact, if you had even taken the time to come down from pouting in your high tower, you would have seen your sister is spending most of her wedding night worrying about you."

Sophia inhaled sharply in surprise at the thought. Her eyes flew to Mina. Her sister stood by Larus but was staring at her. Mina gave her a questioning look, lifting her hand from Larus's arm as if she might step forward. Sophia instantly lifted her hand to stop her, forcing a smile. Mina stayed back, but she didn't look convinced.

Leaning over, she took Malak's goblet from the table and took a sip. The stout liquor choked her on the way down and she coughed violently. Malak leaned into her, blocking her from most of the hall's view.

"Maybe you should try the wine instead," he said, patting her back. "This drink is too strong for humans."

Sophia glared at him. She took the goblet back up and took another sip. It was a mistake. It burned worse than the first time and she ended up coughing again as Malak kept her from the hall's view.

When she could once more focus her watery eyes, she realized that in her coughing fit, she'd leaned over Malak's lap. His thighs shifted and she saw the protrusion of his erection lifting his tunic. She'd witnessed some of the knights in such a state, but they didn't look quite that large. Maybe it was because she had too close of a view.

"Not that I mind you down there, love," Malak said, his voice teasing, "but this isn't the place for such things —at least not until much later and after many more cups have been poured."

Sophia instantly sat up in her chair, leaning away from him. "Go away."

"I can't," Malak said.

"Yes, you can. I'll dance with the next lycan that asks me. Your mission is done. I'll pretend to have a good time."

"Great," Malak said, standing.

When he didn't walk away, she glared at him. "Well? Go away. Run along now, man-beast."

"Dance with me," he said. It sounded more like a command.

Sophia made a face of disgust. "I'll dance with the next man. Not you."

Malak's features clouded for a brief moment before a grin spread over his face. Sophia's stomach knotted. That mischievous, vengeful look couldn't bode well for her.

Malak cleared his throat, lifting his hands to the crowd. Yelling over the music, he called, "One moment, please."

Sophia paled, glancing from him to the crowd. The music stopped and everyone was looking at them. She felt on display as the eyes of those in the hall searched her. Almost fearfully, she returned their stares. What was Malak going to do?

"I would like to announce that Lady Sophia has given me the right of pursuit. Soon, she will be marked as my lover," Malak announced. Good-natured grumbling ensued from the men. "Let any who dare to challenge me step forward."

Sophia instantly shot to her feet, intent on challenging his claim by running away. Malak artfully grabbed her before she could escape and pulled her to his chest. The warm contact stunned her to silence.

"Think of your sister," Malak whispered, his lips brushing close to her temple. Sophia's eyes darted to

Mina who was staring at her in confusion. Then, louder, Malak told the crowd, "The poor, sweet lady is scared of being bitten, but found she couldn't quite resist me and has agreed to the pursuit."

His arrogant tone seemed to add, *How could any woman resist me?*

The men laughed, cheering and howling. Sophia tried to push away from where he had her pulled to his muscular side.

"Yo—" she started to scream.

Malak seemed to anticipate her outrage and crushed his lips to hers to stop it. Liquid desire ran through her body from his touch. For a second, as she quieted, she felt him moving as if to pull back. She hesitantly parted her lips. His mouth changed course and was instantly back on hers, deepening the kiss. Sophia moaned softly as his bold tongue slipped between her lips. He caressed her mouth, plundering its depths.

Slowly, the sound of howling and cheering invaded her numb brain and she struck his arm. How dare he use her to boast to his friends. Malak pulled back, his gray-green eyes once more swirling with hints of gold. He was breathing hard and the unmistakable length of his arousal was pressed to her stomach.

"Now," he whispered, his voice a rough growl, "the

men won't bother you. Your sister won't worry about your mood and—"

"Why?" she broke in, studying his face. Her heart was beating fast. Why did he have to kiss her like that? Why did he have to awaken her body? She didn't want to feel anything right now. She wanted to be numb. She wanted her heart hard and her body insensitive.

"Because my king asked me to speak to you and try to cheer you so that his queen may enjoy her feast," he said. "Obviously, there is no pleasing you and this was the only way I could think of to make everyone happy. You should be pleased as well. No other will dare talk to you for fear of angering me. This also ends any chance I have of finding company tonight unless you by some miracle soften up. No doubt my obvious discomfort in not having someone to warm my bed will please you since you seem to revel in the discomfort of others. And, now you have the protection of two lords. King Larus and myself."

Sophia gasped. He was only kissing her as a favor to Larus? The words were like a splash of cold water over her heated flesh.

Before she could pull away, he loosened his hold and said, "Don't worry, I have every intention of escorting you to the portal."

"I'm going to speak to Larus," Sophia quipped. "I'll get another escort. Your behavior is unacceptable."

"I am your escort. The portal is on my land and I know the way. Larus won't let just anyone have the location of it. Besides, I know the wizard that guards it and I'm the only one who can get you past the gate." Malak moved to touch her face, brushing back her hair as if tenderly caressing her. His words were hard though, belying the affectionate show he put on for the crowd. "So, either behave yourself and let the pursuit stand for the time being and put up with my company. Or I can bite you on your pretty little neck, mark you as my soon-to-be lover and you can spend the rest of your time in this realm feeling deeply connected to me—a connection that will only be broken after we consummate the bond and then later agree to the breaking of it."

"I'll go with the first option," Sophia said, weakly. Truthfully, she was a little scared of being bitten. But looking at Malak, she was more afraid of feeling anymore drawn to him than she already was. "The pursuit thing you said."

"Good choice," he assured, finally releasing her arm. His face had looked pleasant the whole time and remained so as he grinned and lifted his cup toward the king. Larus nodded once and whispered to his wife. Mina smiled, waving slightly at Sophia with an expression of hope on her face. The look tore at her. How could she deny what Malak had done when her sister seemed to get so much pleasure from it?

"What do I have to do?" Sophia asked quietly, staring at her sister's happy face as Larus kissed her cheek. It took everything in her not to let tears spill from her eyes.

"Simple," he said. "Dance with me."

5

DANCE WITH ME.

Malak should have known better. There was nothing simple about that request, nor the effort it took to get her to agree to a song. Two played before she finally forced herself to get up with him.

He was on fire for the shrewish mortal. Watching her slender body turn and bow to him wasn't helping to put the fire out. If anything, his arousal only stiffened all the more and he felt the beast emerging within.

Sophia tried to act like she hated dancing, but he caught a glimpse of pleasure on her face. Perhaps she didn't realize how well lycan eyes could see in the dim light, that he could detect each subtle shift of her features, each shiver of her body. Or how his nose could pick up the scent of her desire, how he knew the instant she became aroused by his nearness.

Or how the others could speak through the mind link and were now using it to tease him mercilessly. Malak blocked them out as his lids fell heavy over his eyes. He stared at Sophia's breasts, watching them jiggle when she gave a little hop. This was torture, pure torture. Finally, the music stopped. Sophia dutifully curtsied to him and moved to walk away. Malak frowned, reaching for her arm.

"Dance with me again," Malak said.

"No."

No? That was all he received? A flat, unemotional, bored *no* like she'd given every other lycan in the palace?

"Come on," he insisted, giving her his most charming smile and seductive tone. "You know you enjoyed it."

"Which part would that be, Lord Beast?" Sophia asked. "You staring at my chest? Or you stepping on my toe because you were too busy staring at my chest?"

Malak frowned. Had he...? No. "I didn't step on your toe."

"Ah, but you did have to think about it," Sophia said. "It may be dark in here, but I could still see your eyes well enough."

"I was thinking that you were too skinny," Malak said. She was skinny, but it wasn't as disgusting as his tone made is sound. Though she could stand to put on a few pounds, she was far from repulsive.

Sophia's expression fell some and he was instantly sorry for his words. Who knew she'd be sensitive about her weight? Nothing else seemed to get through to her, except for her sister. He didn't have time to retract his words as Larus and Mina joined them, cutting off the conversation. Larus lifted a brow at Malak and he heard the king's voice through the mind link, *'What are you about, Malak?'*

'Doing my best not to strangle this one. She is infuriating,' Malak answered dejectedly, knowing Larus wouldn't take him seriously. Mina looked at him as soon as he said it. The mind link was a telepathic connection that all lycans shared. It was the only way they could communicate in their shifted form. Humans couldn't hear it unless mated to a lycan. Then, the human would become connected as well. Malak glanced down at Mina, watching her face. *'Can she hear us yet?'*

'Larus assures me you will take my sister to the portal unharmed,' Mina's voice answered in his head. Larus smirked. Mina glared at him. *'God help you if I find out that you have not.'*

'Yes,' Larus said, a little late. *'She picks up some.'*

"Mina," Sophia said, obviously unaware of the conversation going on around her. She forced a smile for her sister. Mina turned to acknowledge her. "I'm so happy for you."

Malak eyed Sophia as she hugged Mina, lightly kissing her cheek.

'Explain to your wife that I meant no harm by my words,' Malak directed to Larus, doing his best to block Mina from hearing it. If she did, she didn't let on as she and Sophia talked quietly.

'I will,' Larus assured him. *'You have given your word to protect her and I know you will.'*

Malak nodded. Mina hooked Sophia's arm and they stepped away. Malak watched Sophia's backside as she moved.

'You like her, don't you?' Larus said. There wasn't any accusation in his voice, just amusement.

'Who? The shrew?' Malak snorted.

'You know, it would please my wife greatly if Sophia had a reason to stay in our world.' Larus grinned, not needing to say anymore. If Mina were pleased, he'd be pleased.

"Then perhaps you should convince one of these lycans to court her," Malak answered quietly. "Tell them to bring plenty of weaponry for they will need it."

"I have tried to find her suitors," Larus said. "She has turned them all down."

At that, Malak couldn't help but grin.

"Besides, it's a little hard now that you have evoked the right of pursuit. I don't think any of them wish to go up against the legendary Malak, especially when she's shown none but you favor."

"Thanks, my king," Malak said, giving him a mischievous look. "I so do love having your permission to bed your new sister."

Malak bowed and began to walk away, looking for Sophia where he'd seen her disappear into the crowd.

'Malak,' Larus said as he walked away, *'that is not what I said.'*

'And yet that is what I heard,' Malak answered mischievously, rotating in a circle to salute impishly to his friend without breaking stride.

"That was some kiss," Mina said, pulling Sophia by her arm toward the outside bonfire.

Sophia eyed her sister warily. "It was just a kiss."

"Since when do you even allow a man that much? I remember Sir Rupert trying to kiss you. You nearly disemboweled him." Mina laughed, leading the way to the bench where they could talk alone.

"There was no knife on the table tonight," Sophia defended.

"I know you, sister. You would have found one had you wished to. You must like this Malak."

"Mina, it was just a kiss. I let him pursue me so the others would not. It's as simple as that." Sophia hated seeing the hope in Mina's eyes fade, but she refused to lie to her.

"Then...?"

"No, I have not changed my mind. Lord Malak will escort me back to the portal and I will go home as planned." Sophia took a deep breath, trying not to think of the fear she felt at being in the human world without her sister.

"There is no reason to hurry off," Mina insisted.

"There is for me," Sophia said. "I can't sleep here. I can't think. Every little sound makes me jump. With every drink of wine or bite of food I find myself worrying that it is laced with something that will take away my will. I don't want to leave you, but I can't live like this. I want to go home."

"We don't have a home." Mina shook her head. "Not anymore. You know as well as I that our castle was crumbling around our heads. We were going to leave it anyway. What will you do, Sophia? Where will you go?"

"To France like we planned before we were taken," Sophia answered. "I'll dress like a boy and travel like I always wanted to. I may not have money, but I still know how to act like a lady and I can act like a peasant if I need to. When I get to France, they shouldn't care about our father's deeds and surely some nobleman will take a liking to me. Besides, there is always Josephine. She took a liking to me when she visited with her husband. I'm sure she'll introduce me to someone fitting. Even if it is just a Baron or knight."

It was a lie. Sophia had no intention of marrying but knew Mina would be comforted some by the idea. She was right. Mina nodded her head, relaxing some at the plan.

"I wish there were a way we could write," Mina said.

"You learn what you can of magic. I'll look for a sign." Sophia did her best to smile.

"What sign?"

"Some sign that you're trying to communicate to me. If you send it, I'll know it's from you."

"Oh," Mina nodded. "I will try to communicate with you. And will you at least consider staying a while longer?"

"I can't. I've been told the moon here changes. The silver moon turns red and during that time the portals close and none can pass." Sophia sighed. "It's better for me to go now than to wait however long the red moon season lasts."

A tear slipped over Mina's cheek. Sophia hugged her,

unable to hold back her tears. She'd miss her sister desperately, but Sophia knew that she was making the right decision. Over Mina's shoulder, she saw Malak step out into the bailey yard. His eyes met hers and, seeing her with Mina, he nodded and backed away, leaving the sisters be.

6

Malak tried to enjoy himself, but something made him keep looking at the outside door, waiting for the sisters to come back. Feeling Ilar at his side, he turned to see his friend easing down in the chair next to him.

"You don't dance?" Ilar asked, pushing his long hair over his shoulders.

"Can't," Malak said. "Didn't you hear? I had to claim Lady Sophia in pursuit."

"You did?" Ilar laughed. "Sorry I missed that. I was with Rhiannon."

Malak didn't need further explanation. He could well guess what Ilar had been doing with his wife.

"So, you are taken with Lady Sophia?"

"No," Malak lied. Well, it wasn't exactly a lie. He did want her, but he wasn't enamored with her as the right of pursuit would imply. "I did it to put everyone at ease. Larus was worried over Mina. Mina was concerned about Sophia. Sophia was worried that the lycan men would turn her into the main course at a buffet. Larus charged me to take care of the difficult woman, so I took care of it."

"Mm, how noble of you Malak," Ilar laughed. "And here I thought you might desire Sophia."

"Desire? Yes," Malak said. "Have you ever known me not to desire a pretty maid?"

"I'd be lying if I told you this didn't amuse me," Ilar said. "Something tells me you might have met your match at long last."

"It doesn't matter. I promised to see her through the portal and that's exactly what I intend to do." Malak leaned over, grabbed his goblet and downed its contents. As he set the cup down, Mina came in the side door. She instantly went to her husband. Before Malak could stop himself, he was standing. Absently, he said, "I'll talk to you again before we leave."

If Ilar answered, Malak didn't hear it. He knew he'd drunk a little too much, but it was a celebration. Walking out of the hall, he again went to the bailey yard. Earlier, he'd seen the sisters in deep conversation and decided to let them talk. But, now as Sophia would be alone, it was only natural he went to her. After all, he was sworn to protect her until he got her to the portal.

He looked to the bench where he'd last seen the tempting shrew, but she wasn't there. Sniffing the air, he detected her scent and went after her. He found her by the front gate, alone.

"You should come away from there," he said softly.

Sophia jumped at the sound of his voice. She hadn't heard him come up. Reminding himself that she was mortal, he made a mental note to make more noise, so he didn't startle her in the future.

"Go away, Malak," Sophia answered.

"Why do you fight what is between us?" Malak frowned, more at himself than at her. By all the lycan, why did he say that? It sounded so intimate. He must have had more to drink than he'd realized. "What I meant to ask is why do you fight the attraction between us?"

At that she turned, eyeing him. "There is no attraction between us, Malak."

Was that a challenge? He saw the stubborn tilt to her chin, her beautiful face cast in the silvery moonlight. Stepping forward, he reached for her jaw. Her pulse jumped. She could deny it all she wanted, but she was attracted to him.

Malak licked his lips, fighting the wild urgings of the

beast within him. Slowly, he lowered his mouth to hers. Just as he was about to claim her in a kiss, she whispered, "Is this what your honor calls protecting me or did Larus ask you to come out here and try to seduce me?"

"I'm here because I want to be," he answered, his tone as low and very hoarse with his need to lay claim to her.

"You're here because you hope I have softened toward you. You're here only because you wish for a woman to ease your discomfort and warm your bed. You're not here for me. You're here for yourself." Sophia turned her face to the side, not backing away from his touch, just cutting him off. "You're here because you're nothing more than a rutting beast."

Malak dropped his hand and took a step back. Sophia refused to look at him. Her body was stiff and her features hard.

Very quietly, he said, "Be ready to go at dawn. I should hate for that portal to close and lock you here until the next silver moon."

Sophia gasped, eyeing him. "Dawn?"

"Just so we are clear, there is one thing we both seem to agree on," Malak growled. His body was tight with unspent passions. He was not a man used to denying himself. "We both want you out of the magic realm and where you belong as soon as possible. Be ready at dawn."

Malak stiffly nodded to her and stalked away. Going along the outer bailey's wall, he found a notch in the stone and murmured an incantation. The wall parted to let him through.

Once outside the castle wall, it closed once more. Vines grew over the crevices in the uneven gray stone, sprouting little blue flower buds over the surface. It was darker outside the castle walls, but Malak could see just fine. He looked around the forest, detecting some wildlife in the trees, but nothing to worry over.

Looking down, Malak tensed. His erection was so stiff and swollen that it felt like it was about to burst. He turned to the wall, resting his forehead against the cool stone, hoping it would help ease him. At first, he tried to will the erection away. When that didn't work, he licked his hand, wetting it before he lifted the draping tunic to grab his shaft in his fist. The saliva helped his fingers glide over the distended flesh.

It was almost embarrassing, having to relieve himself by his own hand when there were so many women nearby. Usually women were lined up to do it for him—sometimes two or three of them at a time—their mouths and bodies opened for his pleasure, eager to take him any way he wanted. Once, centuries ago, he'd even had as many as six lycan women in his bed. Malak prided himself on being able to please them all.

He kept his head against the wall, imagining Sophia on her knees before him—submissive and compliant, maybe even tied with her hands behind her back as his prisoner. Oh, yeah. That was good. Tied naked and moaning, no *desperately begging*, to suck him with her pouty lips. Malak would never bind her for sex without permission, but a fantasy was a fantasy and this was definitely agreeable to his drunken mind.

Lycans weren't like humans. His kind embraced their sexuality, enjoyed it. There was no shame in finding mutual pleasure. Humans were taught to fear and deny their carnal desires. It was one of the things that had caused the human wars long ago. Humans had been scared, and envious, of the sense of freedom immortals possessed. Lycans had all lived long enough to know that pleasure should be taken where it was found.

He thought of Sophia's rejection and scowled. Why was it he'd forgotten that part of human nature? Sure the women were soft, but some of them could also make a lot of unnecessary work to get them to into bed. Then, there were the others, who easily jumped into bed with whoever would take them. Only afterward, if they were found out, they'd scream ravishment and a whole village would be willing to die to defend the woman's honor.

Malak had been chased by angry villagers many times in the old days when the realms merged freely. At the time, he thought it amusing. The women had been willing enough before they were caught, usually propositioning him to their beds. He'd never once taken an unwilling woman. To do so would be to scar his honor.

In his irritation over being denied physical pleasure by Sophia, Malak stroked himself hard. Squeezing, he pumped his hips, as if he could punish her by taking himself roughly as if it was her mouth he was plunging into and not his tight fist. His breath became harsh and he felt his body partially shifting. He growled viciously in the back of this throat, willing the end to come. It did, wetting the side of the wall.

Malak sighed, taking deep breaths. His drunken mind held on to the pleasure, taking its time coming back to reality. The pressure was gone, but he still felt unsatisfied. Taking a deep breath, he moaned. Why did he have a sinking suspicion that he would be doing this often in Lady Sophia's company?

7

THE SUN WAS BARELY OVER THE HORIZON WHEN Sophia said farewell to her sister. It was a tearful parting, but she knew there was no other way for her. As she had passed through Lycaon's main hall for the last time, she had seen the eyes of the lycan males on her. Their gazes were hot with barely tempered passions. Only Malak's presence at her side, disagreeable as it was this morning, seemed to keep them from approaching. That was at least one thing to be grateful for, even if she would have preferred anyone but Malak to be her traveling companion.

Malak kept a fast pace. She was surprised that no others were with them, but Mina assured her that Malak would behave himself. Sophia wasn't worried about him assaulting her, so much as she was worried about the way he looked at her and tried to seduce her. It had been hard enough to resist in a keep full of people who could happen by, but alone? In the dark? No one around to witness what they did?

Sophia glanced over her shoulder as they walked in silence. The front gates of Lycaon were only specks on the distant horizon. Malak had handed her a pack to carry, keeping one for himself. They walked along a thick forest of red trees. Large, pale leaves graced the branches. Aside from the coloring, the forest looked like those back home. The sky was an odd shade of purple, but the sun was bright and yellow as she was used to.

The forest slowly tapered off, leaving them to nothing but a long open field of rolling grasses. A gentle wind swept over them. Malak only wore a blue tunic tied around his waist and short leather boots. He looked unaffected by the chilly weather. Sophia had on a long-sleeved undertunic dress made of thin linen, a thicker draping tunic of red wool, short boots, and she was trying not to shiver each time the breeze hit her.

Rhiannon had given her a leather strap to bind back her hair. She did so, rolling it all to the nape of her neck to keep it off her face. Still, strands of blonde managed to blow loose, occasionally whipping across her eyes. She glanced at Malak. His raven black hair flowed freely behind him, with the sides bound back from his face. If he weren't so aggravating, she would have thought him handsome. But he was infuriating, having done nothing more than grunt at her a few times in his ill temper before leaving. Now he wasn't even paying attention to her.

"Wouldn't it be faster if you shifted and gave me a ride?" Sophia asked. "Mina mentioned that's how your kind normally travel with humans. It seems to me it would be a lot quicker."

"My lady," he answered, his tone as mocking as his look. "Are you suggesting you would like to straddle me with your thighs and ride me?"

Sophia felt the blood rushing out of her face. Malak didn't even bother to smile.

"Actually, thinking on it," she quipped, "you'd probably only infest me with fleas. That or try to eat me."

"Oh," he tipped his head back and pretended to laugh. There was no humor in the harsh sound though. "You're much too small a meal to bother with."

Sophia stiffened. That was the second time he'd mentioned her weight. Without thought, she responded, "Well, my lord, you would be thin too had the king ransacked your home, killed your father and almost everyone else you knew since childhood as you watched from the distance. Leaving you to spend the next two years starving because you were a lady and ladies have no reason to learn how to hunt for food."

Sophia didn't even bother to keep the bitterness out of her voice. Growing up, she'd begged to go hunting with her father and the knights. She'd even tried to talk him into giving her a falcon. He'd refused, giving her an extensive lecture on a woman's place in a man's home. Her father was a good man, Sophia loved him dearly, but he hadn't prepared his daughters to deal with the consequences of his actions.

"Though I suppose, being a man, you think I should have become the king's mistress like he wanted. I'd be a whore, but at least I'd eat, right? And then maybe I wouldn't appear so offensively small to you." Sophia pressed her lips tightly together, walking faster to get away from him.

He let her be for a moment, before asking, "Did that happen to you?"

"What does it matter," Sophia answered, already cursing herself for revealing so much to him. The last thing she wanted was Malak feeling sorry for her, or thinking she was weak. Actually, it would be better if he stayed irritated with her. When he was annoyed, he wasn't trying to seduce her with his charming smile and wicked looks. "The past is done and I don't feel like discussing anything about myself with you."

"You told me," he growled in irritation. "I didn't ask."

Sophia merely glared at him. Neither one of them said another word on the subject and hours passed in hostile silence.

When her stomach growled, Malak handed her a big chunk of dried meat from his pack. They ate as they moved, drinking water out of a pouch. The field gradually thinned as they neared a wide rocky path. The rolling field turned into small hills. The small hills grew into larger foothills. And, as the day turned into evening, the foothills finally rose in the distance to show a range of glorious mountains. Not entirely unaffected by the magnificent sight, Sophia tried not to make her awe over the beautiful landscape too apparent.

"We camp up here," Malak said, pointing up the hillside to a rock clearing cut into the cliffs. "The high rock face will protect us from the wind during the night."

"We're stopping?" she asked in surprise. "There are still a couple of hours of travel time. The moon's full. I say we keep going."

"At this pace we'll be there in maybe a half a sennight's time," Malak said. "You should conserve your energy."

Sophia hadn't thought to ask how long it would take. She assumed they would maybe camp a night, two at most. "A half sennight? How long if you shifted?"

"I can make the run from Lycaon to Fenris in little over a night. Lycans can run faster at night because the air is different. It would be longer if I ran by day."

Sophia couldn't see spending night after night with Malak. She nervously looked around. Then, biting her lip, she said, "That's not acceptable."

"What?" His eyes rounded as he looked her over.

"That is too long. I need to get back. Look at the moon. It is a little redder, I think. We should try to make better time." Sophia took a deep breath. "You don't want to be with me. I don't want to be with you. We obviously have no liking for each other's company. I say you shift and we bear each other's touch long enough for you to get me to the portal."

"Do you find my presence so distasteful?" Malak asked.

"Yes," she answered, not giving herself time to feel guilty about lying.

"Do you know what? You're right." Malak threw up his hands. "I don't want to deal with you for a second longer than I have to. I should have run you to the portal last night."

"Maybe you should have."

"Fine," he growled, only to shout louder, "Fine." Malak shrugged off his pack and reached for his waist.

Sophia took a step back. "What are you doing?"

He ripped the cloth from around his hips and tossed it at her. Her eyes rounded, seeing his naked body clearly in the silvery moonlight. The shaft between his thighs was halfway raised from a bed of dark hair. As she stared, it only grew stronger, lengthening and becoming thicker. Her body responded and she couldn't look away. She gripped his warm tunic to her chest. It smelled like him.

"I'm shifting to take you back," Malak said. "Unless you wish me to stand here while you continue to look your fill?"

Sophia gasped, instantly turning her eyes away. Nothing she'd ever seen had been so interesting and terrifying at the same time. "I-I..."

"I'll try not to get my fleas on you," he snarled.

Sophia heard a small growl and glanced back. Malak had transformed into a big, black wolf. She took an immediate step back in surprise at how ferocious he looked. Malak's gray-green eyes were gone, replaced by gold. He didn't move as he looked at her.

She'd never looked at a lycan shifted before. The few times she had seen the transformation, she had been under a spell and hadn't noticed how it happened. His body was nearly three times the size of an ordinary wolf. Even as he scared her, the power of his shifted form excited her. Her heart leapt in her chest and her body heated—not so much with desire for the wolf form, but desire for Malak in his human form, knowing he could become this wild beast.

"Malak?" she asked. "Are you in there? Can you understand me?"

Malak lowered his head and lifted one massive paw into the air. She didn't move. He came toward her. She took a step back. He kept walking, his head down until he reached her. His head brushed her outer thigh, lifting slightly in a friendly gesture. Sophia gasped in awe, slowly leaning over to touch his head. His fur was soft and warm. She turned more fully to him, touching him with both hands.

Malak made a small growling sound in the back of his throat, not threatening, just a soft noise. His head turned and he nudged his nose between her thighs, sniffing deeply. Sophia gasped, instantly knowing what he was sniffing for. The low growl turned into a much more wicked sound as he pressed up into her, doing it again.

"Ah," she gasped. Then, coming to her senses, she hit his head several times. "No, bad Malak. Bad."

He whipped back from where he sniffed her sex and seemed to glare at her.

Sophia, realizing she'd yelled at him like a dog, weakly said, "Sorry. I mean, stop doing that."

Malak nodded once and turned his body so his side

was to her. Sophia hesitated and picked up his pack before climbing on. She adjusted her body, resting the best she could along his back with a bent knee over each side of him. Malak stretched, only to lurch into a full sprint. Sophia gasped and held on tight to his fur as the countryside became nothing more than a blur.

Cupid rubbed his gnarled hands together, watching Malak run off with the mortal on his back. Oh, aye. He knew what he had to do. The blonde human would be how he made right his life debt to Malak. It was clear the lycan didn't care for Sophia. Why would he? Her hair was shiny and she had two finely arched brows on her face. Not to mention, she was ugly, smelled like flowers and had smooth skin.

Ugh.

No pustules or scabs. No liver spots or protruding lesions. No hairy moles or rashes. Cupid would never understand how the species of humans managed to breed with creatures as hideous as Sophia.

Ach.

Cupid had kept a close eye on them all day, watching them as they left Lycaon with the dawn. It had taken some doing, but he managed to discover that Lady

Sophia was being taken back home to a portal and that King Larus ordered Malak to do it. Lord Malak was usually smiling and laughing, especially when around women, but with this one he was stiff and angry. They hardly spoke to each other and when they did, it was to fight.

This was perfect, for all the reasons he'd kidnapped the human sister in the first place. They were abandoned in the human world. No one looked for them. And, if Larus had ordered Sophia thrown back into the portal, it was clear no one wanted her in the immortal world. Malak would do his duty and take her to the portal, but after that, he'd be free to extract his hatred on her.

Oh, aye, this was the grand gesture he needed to be out of Malak's debt. Malak would send Lady Sophia to the mortal world before the wizard who guarded the portal to complete his mission. Then, Cupid would pull Lady Sophia back into the immortal realm once she had gone through and deliver her back into Malak's hands without the wizard's knowledge. After that, the lycan could freely punish and torture the object of his hatred without anyone knowing.

Cupid picked at his nose, digging deep only to withdraw it covered in snot. Sucking on his finger, he let a smile spread over his flat, wide mouth. This was a good plan. How could Malak refuse to accept such a favor?

Cupid would bring her back to him, making sure to wait until the red moon came, so she was trapped and under Malak's complete control.

Now this was a perfect idea. How could it possibly go wrong?

MALAK RAN LIKE HE HAD NEVER RUN BEFORE. THE feel of Sophia's parted legs against his back, just knowing her sex was pressed close to him, was too much. Her smell was intoxicating, so much so that he could think of nothing else. When he'd pressed his nose into her thighs, mindlessly moving to smell her, it had been all he could do not to pounce on her.

What had he done to be so tortured by the gods?

This was the very reason he'd made her walk in the first place. That, and the secret hope that she might soften enough toward him if he gave her time. He thought by camping at night, just the two of them, it might actually make her come to him. No one would know and they would be able to act on the sexual tension brewing between them. Or maybe it was his tension brewing. Lifting his head, he sniffed. No, she was aroused as well. Malak ran faster.

Coming to a cliff, he stopped, needing her to get off so they could cross. Breathing hard, he felt Sophia shift on his back, but she didn't get up. Jolting his shoulder, he bounced her lightly. She mumbled but still didn't move. Malak focused his attention past her exotic smell. He detected her steady heartbeat, backed by her steady breathing. She was asleep.

Very carefully, he lay down on his stomach, keeping her on his back. Then, letting his body shift back to human form so as not to wake her, he felt her moan and curl alongside his naked back. Malak nearly howled when her leg slipped between his to nestle intimately close. It took some maneuvering, but he managed to slip her gently to the ground next to him. As he pulled away, she moaned in protest.

Malak crouched, studying Sophia as she slept. He pulled absently at his bottom lip in thought, before reaching out to brush a wayward strand of blonde hair from her face. She must have been tired if she fell asleep on him. He did detect little dark circles underneath her closed eyes. It was chilly out and he felt her shiver from the cold.

He grabbed his blue tunic off the ground and looked around. Seeing a small outcropping of rocks, he jumped onto it and laid his tunic on the ground to make a bed. Then, jumping back down, he picked Sophia up, cradled her to his naked body and leapt back onto the ledge with her in his arms. Her eyes opened briefly. A soft smile came to her mouth and then she fell back asleep.

Malak laid her on the bed. Unfastening the knot on her shoulder, he took her overtunic off and lay down next to her taking the spot closest to the ledge, before covering them up. Since he'd used his tunic to cover the ground, he was naked beneath the blanket. Luckily, there was room on the ledge so they didn't have to touch and where they did, her linen undertunic kept his skin from pressing along hers. Malak wasn't sure he could handle much more physical contact.

Stretching out on his back, he threaded his hands behind his head as he looked at the stars. Sophia moaned, turning to rest her head on his chest for a pillow. Malak stiffened, taking a deep breath at the contact. Easing her head from over his heart, he let her use his arm instead, wrapping it along her back to hold her to his side. Not knowing why, he brushed his lips against her forehead, not kissing her, just a light stroke.

Sophia made a soft noise as she continued to sleep,

curling into his warmth. She lifted her thigh onto his. Malak groaned, doing his best not to wake her. He must have done something wrong because the gods were trying to kill him.

9

SOPHIA WIGGLED HER BODY INTO THE WARMTH AT her side. Whatever it was, it felt good, safe. It had been so long since she'd slept, and even longer since she'd truly felt safe, that she didn't want to wake up.

Something hot touched her thigh, working along her flesh to her hip. She wanted it there, stroking her, making her ache. The movements were slow, languid. The heat slid down her leg, pulling at the back of her knee, drawing her closer to the warmth she craved. Sensations flooded her body, coming from every direction—the hand working back up her thigh and rounding toward her butt, the stiff heat pressing through the linen at her stomach, the smell of Malak.

Malak?

"Malak?" she groaned, her voice heavy from sleep. Sophia blinked, opening her eyes. Malak was next to her. At her word, his naked chest pressed closer to her aching breasts causing her treacherous nipples to tingle. Gasping, she tried to shake the fog off her brain. She didn't stand a chance.

Malak's mouth blindly searched for hers, bumping her cheek and drawing over her lips. The press of his kiss was everything she remembered and she was helpless against the deep onslaught of his probing tongue as it invaded her mouth. His hand on her butt kneaded her flesh, pulling her closer as it somehow worked her skirt higher up her waist.

Malak's body twisted and suddenly she was beneath him. Her eyes flew open and she tried to scream. All that came out of her mouth was a long, sultry moan. The feel of his body was wickedly delightful. At the sound of her voice, his eyes flickered open and she saw the gray-green depths slashed with liquid gold before they shut once more.

Raven black hair tickled her and she couldn't resist running her fingers into his silky locks, only to touch his muscled back and chest. He left her lips, moving his mouth to her neck. Animalistic noises left him as he kissed the pulse at her throat.

It felt too good. She didn't want him to stop, didn't think to make him. His whole body rubbed into hers, pressing her against the hard ground. She knew the sensations flooding her female sex. Touching her own body, fantasying with her mind, had never brought her this much pleasure.

Malak's mouth worked kisses along her throat only to devour the other side of her neck. He sucked deeply at her flesh, nibbling, licking, kissing. The hand on her backside moved away and she felt him cupping her sex, parting the sensitive folds as he explored every intimate inch of her. He didn't hesitate as he thrust a thick finger up into her tight passage.

Sophia gasped, her eyes opening wide. Malak groaned, rocking his hand against her, joining the first finger with a second. His mouth left her neck, only to cover her budded nipple as it strained through the linen of her undertunic. He kissed her through the material, sucking and licking and biting. The feel of heat so intimately inside her, pushing in and out, in and out, combined with the workings of his mouth left her lightheaded.

His legs were between hers, keeping her knees parted even as she instinctively tried to close them. Just as she started to feel the strong tingle building in her sex, he pulled his hand away. Sophia moaned in protest, shaking her head back and forth as she wantonly wanted more.

Malak's lips were back on her neck, passionately kissing her skin and his hand massaged her breast. The sensations were too much. She didn't know where to feel or how to react or what to think. The heat came back to part her sex, focusing her mind on that one point on her body, but this time the heat was thicker and harder than before.

Seconds before it happened, Sophia realized what this meant. Malak was about to stake claim to her maidenhead. She moaned, but it was too late to protest. Her hands were gripping his shoulders. Her thighs were parted to him and his body was poised at her entrance.

With a rough thrust he was embedded inside her. Malak growled, pulling back only to push his shaft deeper with another thrust. Her legs tensed. He did it again, each time seating himself deeper inside, stretching her, prying her body open to him.

At first it burned, the pain overtaking the pleasure, but as Malak kissed her neck, she felt a strange euphoria taking the pain away. He growled in the back of his throat, a possessive, territorial sound that gave her a small sense of satisfaction. His hand slid from her breast and he braced both palms on the ground. His knees pushed up, angling her hips to deepen his already penetrating thrusts. His hips worked against her. He rode her, controlling her.

Despite the almost brutal, primitive way he moved, it felt wonderful. She arched into him, accepting his claim. Tension built between her thighs and she didn't want it to stop.

Sophia opened her eyes, gasping to find his face partially shifted. Crimson blood stained his mouth and chin, and she saw his sharpened fangs. His muscled body worked as he took her hard. She was too far gone with arousal to care. Her body spasmed, tightening as it clamped down on his thrusting shaft. She gasped as the most breathtaking yet tumultuous feelings assaulted her entire body. Nothing in her world had ever felt like this.

As she stiffened, Malak grunted and joined her. His back arched, his hips flush against hers, as he groaned, jerking his release inside her. Sophia felt as if she couldn't breathe. Malak collapsed on top of her, bracing his weight with his bended knees and elbow as not to crush her as the harshness of his breath fanned over her neck. The position of his body kept her trapped beneath him and he stayed embedded deep inside her.

As the pleasure subsided, reason slowly dawned.

Sophia stiffened, her eyes flying open as she drew her arms back as if his flesh would burn her alive. Weakly, she touched her throat, remembering the blood on his mouth. Warm sticky fluid met her hands on both sides of her neck. Sophia did the only thing she could think of. She screamed.

10

Malak was mindless, content to stay deep into the soft folds of the woman's body. No, not just any woman. Sophia. She'd accepted him. The details were foggy, but he was inside her and she had not resisted his claim to her.

Then she screamed, the piercing sound of fear and outrage ringing through his head. Malak's whole body jerked. He pushed up and away from her, torn between the need to protect her and the desire to stay close to her. He looked around for the thing that scared her. A dragon flew overhead and he relaxed.

A smile starting to form, he turned to look down at her. Malak was sure his whole life ended in that one moment. Sophia lay on the ground. Her gown was pushed up around her waist. She was pale, shaking, and worst of all she was covered in blood. The bite marks on her neck were unmistakable, as was the tiny mark on her breast. Not only that, but there was also a smudge of blood on her thigh. Closing his eyes, he tried to remember that first thrust into her sweet, tight body. Torment rolled over him. There was no mistaking it. She'd been pure.

He'd been so tempted by her, having smelled her desire for him from that first moment. She'd denied him, fought him and then in sleep she'd cuddled into his arms, sighing his name over and over as if calling to him in a dream. Malak had refused to take advantage of her, but then she had touched him, her small hand rubbing his chest and stomach and hips. She'd been moaning by that point.

Thinking back on it now, she determined it was possible she'd been sleeping when she'd done it. By all the lycan, *he'd* been sleeping when it started. Malak had denied himself pleasure and the beast inside him must not have been too happy about it. How could he not remember the beast coming out? How could he not remember biting her, marking her so thoroughly that he'd done it in three spots?

Sophia glanced over her body, only to look at him again. Her mouth opened as she screamed—not at the dragon, but at him. She jerked to standing, wobbling on her feet. Malak lifted his hand, wanting to reach for her. When he tried, she'd pulled back from him, stepping dangerously close to the edge.

"How dare you." she screeched.

"Sophia, please, step away from the ledge, you're going to hurt yourself. I know what you're thinking, but the wounds are already healing. It's not as bad as you think. I can explain."

"Not as bad as I think?" she yelled. "You marked me."

Malak stiffened. Huh? That wasn't what he was expecting her to be upset over.

"You did, didn't you?" Sophia glared at him, seeming oddly unconcerned with the fact that he'd taken her body like she was a woman used to receiving such passion, or the fact that she'd been bitten by a wild beast. No, she was mad because he marked her with his scent so everyone would know she was his. "You marked me. Now I'm going to be having feelings for you, aren't I? Oh, why did you have to do that? I don't like you, Malak. I don't want to be connected to you. I don't want to be connected to anyone. Argh. How could you do this…? *Argh*."

"So you're mad that I marked you as my lover?" Malak asked, trying to wrap his brain around it.

"Have you not been listening?" she growled. Shaking

her head and muttering curses at him, she grabbed her tunic and began struggling to put it on. "I'm tired of being forced to feel."

"But, your...?" He gestured helplessly at her stomach. It had been so long since he'd even thought of a virgin, let alone had one in his bed. Had he ever had one in his bed? He honestly couldn't recall a time.

"Maidenhead?" she supplied when he couldn't form the word, only to grimace at him like he was an imbecile for asking. "I don't care about that. I had no intentions of keeping it forever and since I won't marry, it seems a little silly to get worked up over how it was lost."

"Then you were?" He frowned, placing his hands on his hips. The more he thought about it, he was starting to get upset. So he was good enough to pleasure her, but not good enough to have marked her?

"Ugh, focus," she demanded, her tone condescending. She grabbed his tunic and threw it at him. Malak automatically tied it around his waist. "I need you to take the mark thing away. What do we do? Both agree that it needs to be gone. Okay, I want it gone."

Malak's jaw tightened.

"It's your turn," Sophia prompted, arching a brow. "Will it away. I don't want to be claimed by you."

He could hardly breathe, let alone speak.

"It doesn't work like that, does it?" she asked when

he didn't say the words. "Great. Just bloody great. You know, you're all alike. You want me to bend to your will, be your little lovesick woman pining over you. Ah, but I'm ahead of you this time. I'll fight it. Any tender thing I should start to feel for you, which I don't right now, I'll be able to resist. This is one human who's not going to—"

"The portal's up ahead," Malak stated coldly, interrupting her tirade. He didn't want to hear anymore. She'd made her point perfectly clear. The sooner he shoved her through to the other side the better. Already he felt a connection to her, one he didn't like one bit.

Hopping off the ledge, he began to walk. Sophia gasped at his abrupt dismissal, but Malak ignored her. Anger and rage boiled in his chest. He was good enough to sleep with her, but not good enough to mark her as his lover. What, did she have others lined up? Was there someone else? It had been mentioned the vampire Lord Devlin had interacted with her. Did she pine for that bloodsucker?

The way she spat at him, hating him with every word, every hard look, tore at him. He'd never felt more pleasure in a woman's body and she could barely stand to be in his presence. Sure, she might desire him, had let him use her body, but she didn't even like him. In fact, she seemed to think she was better than he was as if he'd insulted her by marking her in such a possessive way.

By all the lycan, three bites.

One bite was a strong mark, but three? Three would ensure that no one touched her from his world. Three would bind her to him so tight that he'd hurt physically if he tried to bed anyone else. Actually, he couldn't even think of another he wanted to bed.

Malak walked faster, hearing Sophia stumble to keep up. He had to get her through that portal. Only when she was far away from him, would he be back to his old self.

Sophia walked behind Malak, her whole body shaking. She was mad, scared, sad, terrified. Already she felt her body trying to connect to him, reaching for him, desiring him. Even as her insides ached from where he'd taken her, she wanted him to do it again.

The bites didn't scare her. They didn't hurt and Mina had recovered from hers just fine. She was never one to pretend she was in pain when she was not. What scared her was that he'd marked her, was trying to enchant her to him, take away her will. Had he wanted her permission, he'd have asked her first. But, no, he just did it, trying to take her spirit away from her—just like those before him.

Tears flooded her eyes, but she dashed them away. This is exactly what she feared would happen if she stayed in the magic realm. Sophia didn't want to feel anything tender, not even caring or a simple attachment. She wanted her freedom.

The path narrowed as they worked their way up the side of a mountain. Sophia glanced down the steep incline, hugging along the cliff wall. It looked like the path only got smaller and smaller, disappearing into the flat surface. There was nowhere to go but down. Looking over the edge, she briefly thought about jumping. Just as quickly, she dismissed it. She was never one to take the easy way out. Her stomach dropped from looking down too long.

"Here." Malak turned back to her and reached out his hand as if sensing her sudden plight. "Take my hand."

Sophia instantly pulled back, not reaching for him. She couldn't touch him, not now, not ever.

His face darkened. "Fine. Just try not to fall. I would hate to have you stuck here."

"Well, I'd hate to be stuck here," she snapped. "In fact, can we hurry this up?"

Malak growled, snarling at her. He continued along the ledge only to stop after a few feet. Running his hand over the face of the mountain, he quickly whispered some words, growling them in his native tongue. Sophia couldn't understand them and didn't even try to.

She looked out over the distance. The view was

beautiful. Mountains poked out over the distance, meeting the clear purple sky. Hearing a noise, she glanced back at Malak. He was gone. Panicking, she called, "Malak? Malak!"

His hand shot out of the side of the mountain as if coming right out of the stone. She inched toward it, eyeing his moving fingers. Hesitantly, she touched him to see if it was real. His fingers snaked around her wrist and jerked her into the side of the mountain. She yelped as she fell through the stone like it was air only to hit Malak's solid chest. He instantly grabbed her by her upper arms and set her back from him.

Sophia found herself inside the mountain. When she turned around, whatever door she'd come through was gone. In its place, the walls of a cave sparkled like she was inside a gemstone. Colorful stalagmites grew from the floor, outlining a single path that led deeper into the mountain. Ridges of dripstone formed crystals across the ceiling, hanging into the occasional stalactites.

"Where is that light coming from?" Sophia looked around, unable to see a fire.

"The portal," he answered, walking so fast she had to jog to keep up with him. "Come on. It's this way. Try not to fall over the side."

Sophia looked down. Along each side was the stalag-mites formed a rail of sorts to keep her from falling over.

The path was narrow and she had to remain behind Malak. She was drawn to look at his bare back. Long strands of his dark hair bounced lightly along his spine. Malak stopped as they neared the end of the cave passageway and she was so transfixed by his body that almost bumped into him.

"Merrlyn," Malak called through the door.

"Yea, Lord Malak, I've been expecting you," a weathered voice answered. "Come in. Introduce me to your woman."

Sophia stiffened.

"Oh, she doesn't like being called your woman," the same voice said with a laugh. "And yet she carries your teeth marks on her neck."

Sophia gasped in surprise, lifting to touch her neck. She looked around but could detect no tiny creatures watching them. "How does he see this?"

Suddenly, an old man appeared to match the weathered voice. He wore a plain green tunic over his slender, hunched frame, and a long gray beard grew over his chest matching the wiry locks of his hair. Wrinkles looked as if they'd laid siege to his face centuries ago.

"At eight hundred and ninety-eight, let's see if you look as good as me, mortal," the wizard laughed.

"Merrlyn, this is Lady Sophia," Malak said. "King Larus has ordered—"

"Larus?" Merrlyn interrupted. "He's king of the lycans now?"

"For some time, yes," Malak said.

"Hmm, I might have heard that somewhere. The rocks aren't that great for gossip, you know. But they do tell me what I need to know." The wizard motioned to his side. Malak stepped into the chamber, giving her room to follow. She looked at the wall Merrlyn had motioned to. Like a live painting, an image of outside the cave came to them. If she looked hard enough, she could see the speck of land where Malak had made love to her. Her cheeks reddened. It hadn't even occurred to her that someone could have been watching.

"I closed my eyes," the wizard assured her.

Sophia couldn't look at him. Her humiliation was complete. The rest of the wizard's chamber was like the entrance to the cave. Odd furniture had been made from the stone formations. There was a narrow bed on a ridge, a chair and tables made of stone, and even a torch stand carved into one of the stalagmites.

"Please, kind sir," Sophia said. "I want to go home. I'm told you have a portal."

"Where are you from? Italy?" The wizard cocked his head to the side to study her. "You don't look like the Italians. Saxon, perhaps? Norse?"

"Wessex. I'm from Wessex," she said. "But I'll take

France if you have it, or anywhere really, so long as it's my world and not this one."

Malak grunted and she tried her best to ignore him. It didn't work. She felt his eyes on her and she had to look at him. His handsome face etched itself on her memory. Since this was the last time she would ever see him, she found it hard to hate him quite as much as she ought to.

"My lord," she whispered, holding out her hand. "You've kept your bargain and I thank you. Please, give my love to my sister should you see her again."

A tear slipped over her cheek. Malak nodded once but didn't speak. She turned from him.

"I can't remember a France," the wizard said. "Ah, well, I'll do a birthplace spell. That should get you close enough. Your family didn't move around, did they?"

Sophia shook her head. "No. It's just me. I don't care where you put me."

"Ah, well then, go on if you're in a hurry." The wizard again motioned to the moving painting on the cave wall.

Sophia looked at it and gasped. It was her home. Winter snow lay thick and white over the crumbling walls of the castle. She'd forgotten about the cold that awaited her. The front gate was smashed to pieces by a battering ram from the siege and the high towers of the keep had holes from the king's catapults. A cold breeze hit her as she stared at the cave wall.

"Malak," she said, turning to say goodbye. He wasn't there. Only the landscape stretched around her. She gasped in shock. "Malak? Can you hear me? Malak? Malak."

Malak stared at the wall, watching Sophia's body dissolve into it. She didn't look back as she left him through the portal. It was just as well she didn't say anything more to him. As the wall hardened to replace the image of an abandoned castle, he expected the pull he felt for her to lessen. It didn't. His heart tightened in his chest until it threatened to stop beating. He took a deep breath and then another.

"Time," he assured himself. Time would make the pain go away. It had only been a few seconds and he did bite her three times.

"It is a cure for most things," the wizard agreed, "given enough of it."

Malak nodded at the man. Inside he felt empty. The

home Sophia chose to go back to was a horrific place, by any standard. He remembered what she'd said about her father and the human king. By the looks of her home, she was telling the truth. She must truly loathe him and his kind to choose a crumbling, barren castle over the life of privilege Larus offered to give her as his ward. Had she but asked, Malak would have taken her to Fenris and given her a place there as well. Many lycans would willingly marry her, giving her a choice of whatever life she wanted to lead. Here she would have been loved, adored, cared for, tended to, protected. And yet, she chose a pile of rocks and snow.

He looked at the pack he carried. There wasn't much, but there was food in it. "Can I send this behind her?"

"Too late," the wizard said. "She took her location with her."

"You need anything, Merrlyn? Food? Clothes? Supplies?" Malak turned to the man, doing his best to force Sophia from his mind. It wasn't as easy as he had hoped.

"A woman," the old man said, cackling. He asked for one each time Malak saw him.

"That I would not wish on any man," Malak answered, as he always did. "Can't you conjure one to fill the need?"

"That I do," the old man agreed. "Will you be staying for tea, Lord Malak, or do you have to go?"

"I have nowhere to be," he said, staring at the wall in longing. "And no one is expecting me to be there."

12

WESSEX, REALM OF MORTALS, WINTER 1407 AD

Glancing around the familiar landscape of her home, Sophia shivered to see the desolate keep. Upon her arrival back into the mortal realm, she'd walked toward the castle, knowing that there should be firewood gathered by the fireplace. It had been dark inside, but she knew the old stones better than any place between heaven and earth.

As she managed to light a meager fire, Sophia turned to look around. Bowls were set out on a table. It was the meal she and her sister had been eating when Cupid drugged them. Slowly walking to the table, she touched the rim of her sister's bowl. Tears entered her eyes and all she could do was cry.

"Why did I come back to this?" she whispered regretfully. But how could she not? Malak's image came to mind and she shivered. She could still feel his hands on her body.

Suddenly, a horrible, yet familiar smell assaulted her and she turned in horror. Gagging, she said, "Cupid."

The little troll's lips spread into what had to be the scariest smile she'd ever seen. His beady eyes bore into her as he waddled forward on his stubby legs. Sticking his finger up his nose, he itched around in it. Sophia gagged as he stuck the same finger into his ear.

"What do you want? Leave me alone," she demanded.

"Ach, your voice is as ugly as ringing bells," the troll grimaced.

"I said leave me alone. You've done enough." She continued to back away from him. But where could she go? "What do you want from me?"

"It's not a matter of what I want." Cupid reached into his pocket and pulled out a pink vile of liquid. "It's what Lord Malak wants."

Sophia screamed, running full tilt toward the castle door. Something hit the back of her head, but she tried to keep moving. A numbing sensation worked its way over her and her limbs felt heavy. Before she could do anything about it, she was falling toward the floor, her vision darkening.

Not again.

13

FENRIS CASTLE, REALM OF MAGIC

Malak frowned, not wanting to get up from his game, especially not to receive a dirty little troll—a troll he blamed for the torment in his soul, a troll that had brought his tormenter, Lady Sophia, into what he had thought was his perfect world. Now, he was going through the motions of living. It had been five very long days and nights as he watched the silver moon fade into red, sealing the portals. He'd sent a dispatch to Larus upon completing his mission and seeing Sophia through to her world. Malak knew the king would be relieved at the moon's changing, as Cupid could cause no more mischief for the season.

Then what was the horrid little being doing at Fenris? Surely he wanted to thank him for saving his life, but Malak preferred the troll do nothing in return. In fact, he might have left him in the quicksand to drown had he known whose arm it was poking out of the sand.

"He said if you didn't come, he would meet you down in the hall," his steward insisted. The man was slight in stature compared to the lycans, but being part fairy, part elf made Gaston exceptionally well equipped to run Malak's castle for him.

"Argh," Malak grumped, slamming his game piece down on the table. He nodded at Andor, one of his lycan guards. "This game is yours. I forfeit."

Andor laughed and picked up his goblet. "I accept your defeat."

Malak growled good-naturedly at him before turning to follow his steward toward the stairwell. There was no pleasure in him as they walked silently up toward his bedchambers.

"I've already ordered the fairies to change your bedding when he leaves," Gaston said. "Kaatja wanted me to extend her offer to stay in your bed after it is refreshed, should you have need of refreshing yourself."

Malak shook his head in denial. He hadn't been able to think about touching anyone but Sophia since first seeing her in Lycaon. Many of the women of his court were upset, but what could he do? His body still felt a connection to Sophia. If anything, that connection grew to torment him.

The passageways through his castle were dark due to the black stone it was built out of. If he listened carefully, the sound of water could be heard in the distance. It was a stream that ran through the nearby forest. Torches lit the way, their orange glow giving the uneven stone walls an eerie contrast. His bedchamber was in the highest part of the main tower with access to the high roof. He liked spending his nights outside and the view was particularly splendid from the tower's height.

His bedchamber was a large, circular room. A fire burned in the fireplace, an eternal flame always lit by magic like the torches throughout the castle. It was one of the few spells Malak had learned to cast over the years, mainly thanks to Merrlyn. A large trunk was in the corner, near a narrow slit of a window. A stream of red moonlight came from outside. He hadn't realized it was so late. Malak had been too busy trying to find ways of not thinking about Sophia. Even now, it was as if he could feel her presence around him.

Looking at his bed, he grimaced. His steward was right. The bedding would have to be changed. Cupid lounged in the middle of the large mattress, his horrid little body nestled into his favorite blue and silver coverlet. Malak frowned. "What is this about a present, troll?"

Cupid sat up, grinning widely. Somehow the happy expression made Malak apprehensive. If Cupid was happy it usually didn't bode well for anyone around him. "Take care. She understands our language. I got tired of repeating myself so I cast a language spell."

Malak sighed heavily. Cupid gestured to the end of the bed. Something moved within a dirty sack on the floor. "You brought me an enchanted goat?" Malak laughed, though the sound was dark.

"I brought you revenge, my lord," Cupid said, poking a gnarled finger in his ear.

Now Malak was worried. He leaned over to untie the sack. The troll's stench was so great he couldn't smell anything beyond it. At his handling, whatever it was started to kick. Reluctant to reach inside, the lycan pulled the material down to expose a clump of muddy hair.

"Take your anger out on her. No one knows of her presence. I made sure of it." Cupid stood on the bed, jumping lightly in excitement. He clapped his hands. "The perfect compensation for a life debt. The one creature you hate above all others."

As the troll said it, Malak flinched as two startled brown eyes were revealed to him. Sophia glared out at him from her dark, muddy prison. How...?

"Cupid," Malak growled, torn between freeing her

and strangling the troll. He looked up just as the troll was stepping into a small black hole.

Cupid's body was whisked away, but not before he mumbled, "Bah. I am done meddling in the affairs of lycans until they cross me again. If I have to look at one more of those horrifically sweet humans again, I'll retch."

Malak closed his eyes briefly before springing into action. Not caring that she was covered in foul mud or smelled horrible, he grabbed Sophia and began freeing her. Inside the sack her limbs were tied together and her mouth was gagged. Letting a claw form on his fingertip, he cut her free.

Sophia gasped for air, her body slow to move as she rubbed her wrists. Malak reached to help her up, but she hit his hand away. "You." That one word was enough to express all she felt, and she definitely wasn't happy with him.

"Sophia," he said, nodding. His body instantly pulled toward her. He wanted to hold her, to shout with pleasure that she was returned to him—no matter how it came about. Malak lifted his hands, eager to pull her to his chest and demand she never again leave his sight. Life had been hell without her. He'd tried to resign himself to never seeing her again, but now that she was here he knew he could not let her go. His duty was done. It wasn't his fault Cupid had brought her back.

"You," she repeated, her tone hateful. "How could you hire that... that *creature* to kidnap me from my home? Let me guess. You ordered him to enchant me too. That's what that pink stuff was. That's why I can't stop thinking about you, isn't it? You bastard. How could you? All I ever wanted was my freedom, but you couldn't give me that much, could you? Can't you take a hint? I don't want you. I *do not* want to be here. I don't want Larus. I don't want Devlin. And I don't want you."

Malak's gut tightened at her words. Had Cupid tried some sort of spell on her to make her want him? Did he think that by doing so, Malak could better exact revenge on Sophia—whatever that meant? Who knew what went through the twisted little trolls head?

"You think that I am capable of..." He motioned to the sack.

"I want a bath," Sophia announced. She wobbled on her feet. "You can do at least this much for me. I want a bath. I want a change of clothes. And I want to see my sister."

"Your sister is with Larus on their honeymoon," Malak said. "Then he is taking her to meet the elders."

"Then I will wait for her at Lycaon."

"Fine," he growled.

"Fine," she said. He started to walk away. "Hey. What do you think you're doing?"

Turning toward her, his body tight, he bowed. "To get my lady a bath before she stinks up my home."

Malak was torn between intense pleasure and pain. His heart squeezed in his chest. It would seem their time apart didn't cause any tender feelings to grow in her. Sure, she wanted him, admitted to as much, but she didn't like him. She even thought him capable of hurting her. His limbs shook as he thought of her tied up in a bag, covered in mud and gagged. If he ever found Cupid he'd beat him senseless.

Sophia chewed the last of the bread as she slowly lowered her body into the first of two baths of hot water. She was so dirty, Malak had sent up fairies with two tubs as well as a plate of food. Apparently, just like Lycaon, fairies worked in Fenris as maids. The vain little wretches giggled and pointed at her, making a great show of holding their noses. Scrubbing off as much mud as she could, she stood and hurried to get into the second tub where hair rinses and soap awaited her. Unfortunately, the soap smelled like Malak and she had to choose between an intense sexual desire for the frustrating lycan or being dirty. Cleanliness won.

After her bath, she quickly dried off before the fire. The fairies had left her a gown on the bed. It was a long blue piece of material like many of the lycan women wore. Sophia frowned as she tried to wrap it around her body. No matter how she did it, the gown she fashioned didn't cover enough of her flesh. Her arms were bare and her legs poked out from under the skirt. It might be acceptable for lycan women to go about in such a state, but she felt exposed.

While she bathed, she had studied the bedchamber. Undoubtedly it was Malak's. What it lacked in feminine décor it made up for in weaponry. Swords were displayed along the wall, along with some strange looking weapons she'd never seen. Small pouches were lined up along a long table, differing only by the color of their material.

Her eyes fell on a small door in the corner. Slowly, she walked toward it. Behind the door, a long row of stairs led up and she followed them. Her limbs shook and she was tired from her long days with Cupid. The troll had kept her tied up most of the time, at least when she wasn't drugged. Luckily, the troll found her as repulsive as she did him and didn't lay a hand on her, except to smother her "grotesque" face and clothing with stink mud.

The stairwell led to the top of a tower. She hadn't realized she was so high up off the ground. Slowly, she edged toward the side of the battlements. The red moon gave a bloody cast to the land, making her skin look as if it glowed. She could see well beyond the Fenris's front gate. Cupid had made no secret of where he was taking her and she knew this to be Malak's home. There was something gothic to the castle's appearance, almost like a cathedral she'd once seen as a girl, both awe-inspiring and fearful at the same time.

The enclosed stairwell hid a large corner of the roof from view, as it extended into a wall. Walking around the side, she thought to have heard a noise, almost like a long sigh. She debated on whether or not to turn back but finally determined it must have been the wind against the stone.

Still, just to be cautious, she leaned around the edge of the wall to peek. Suddenly, she stopped, gasping in fright. An eyeball about the size of her head awaited her, its dark center dilating beneath its scaly lid. The creature huffed, blowing a small ball of fire from its nose. Sophia felt the dragon's heat as she jumped back, screaming in fright. The sound of her voice must have alarmed the creature, because he too threw back his head and roared, blowing a long trail of fire into the night air.

The creature towered over her as it stood tall, roaring again into toward the stars. It was hard to tell its exact color in the red light, but the creature had dark flesh that ridged into sharp-looking points along its tail and back. Sophia stumbled back, only to be caught against a warm chest. Instantly, she knew it was Malak. A feeling of security washed over her as she turned in his arms. She wiggled, ducking under his arms to hide behind his back.

"Dra..." she tried to speak. "Dr..."

"Dragon," Malak said softly.

"They... hibernate. When Larus was leading us through a forest, a creature said that dragons... sleep." It was all she could eke out, but he seemed to understand. Amazingly, Malak didn't seem afraid.

"They wake up," he answered. Lifting his hand, he said to the creature, "Welcome, old friend."

Sophia realized that they were speaking in the gruff language of the lycan people, but she understood it perfectly as if it were her own. That's one thing she could thank Cupid for—the spell he cast so she could understand all languages.

The dragon snorted, blowing a puff of smoke. "Do the wizards grow humans again to feed us?"

Sophia gasped. She held tight to Malak's bare arm. His chest and back were naked, like always, and she pressed herself to his natural warmth. "Did that thing just...?"

"Talk?" Malak asked.

"Say he wanted to eat me?" Sophia corrected. "And, now that you mention it, yeah, and talk?"

"We did not enjoy the humans last time. Too salty," the dragon snorted. "And definitely too rude."

"Sorry, old friend," Malak said. "Cupid opened the portals between the realms and she's been brought through. She means no offense. Right, Sophia?"

"Ah..." Her mouth worked and she nodded eagerly. "No offense. Yes. No offense."

"Ah, well, keep your woman in line, Malak." The dragon snorted and Sophia got the impression the giant creature was laughing. "I never took you for settling with a mortal, but congratulations to you and the lady of Fenris."

"Oh, I'm not—" she tried to deny. Malak lifted his hand to cover her mouth, pulling her close to his chest. She blinked in surprise as his warmth curled into her.

"She's not been officially announced as my mate," Malak said. "She has yet to accept my proposal."

Proposal? Sophia grimaced. Did he think he was funny, saying such things?

"*Harrumph.* She accepted the marking well enough by the smell of her." The dragon flapped its tail and lifted two very long wings off its back. Sophia hadn't noticed the wings before that moment. She'd been too busy staring at his enormous face. "I never did understand female mortals. I don't think they know what they want."

Sophia frowned. Did her whole race get insulted by

a dragon? Something that spewed fire from its mouth and looked like an overgrown lizard?

Pushing away from his chest, she opened her mouth to defend her human gender. Malak grabbed her arms and pulled her to him once more, planting a hard kiss to her mouth. Sophia moaned in surprise, her whole body melting against him. She'd thought she'd never feel him or taste him ever again. When he held her, all fear seemed to fade away.

Mindlessly giving into the pleasure, she ran her hands over his chest to his neck. Malak lifted her off the ground. Her body pressed tightly to his. Long strands of his hair blew over her shoulders, cocooning her within the silky locks.

Malak pulled his lips away first. His lids heavy, he said, "Excuse us, old friend. Stay as long as you wish. You are always welcome here."

"Aye, go convince her then," the dragon said.

Sophia blinked, her mind coming out of the fog his kiss had weaved around her senses. She struggled to be let go and he set her down. A hard breeze beat across her back and she shivered, turning in time to see the dragon take flight. When it was far off into the sky, she realized Malak's hands were still on her waist. He leaned over, kissing her neck.

She hit him in the arm. "What do you think you're doing? I told you, I don't want you."

"You keep saying that, and yet..." Malak let go of her and took a deep breath. Was he smelling her? She gasped, taking a step away from him.

"I told you, I'm stronger than any enchantment. I won't succumb to you. I don't care what that troll did to me, or hit me with, or what spell he cast. I am a free woman and I make up my mind."

"Not this again," he sighed, leaning against the stone wall. He crossed his arms over his chest. "You are not under a spell and even if you were, I am immune to troll magic. Cupid's little love spells don't work on me. What is between us is real. I saved Cupid's life and he brought you here to repay the life debt."

"Ah-ha. So you did put him up to it because he owed you a favor." Desire pumped through her veins and she wanted desperately to be back in his arms, kissing him, exploring him. "You might be unaffected by his magic, but I know for a fact that I'm not. You made him put a lust spell on me. That's why I want you in my bed."

Malak grinned. It was an impossibly sexy look as his eyes roamed over her length in a slow caress. "He wouldn't have enchanted you because he thinks that I want revenge against you."

"Revenge?" She laughed in disbelief. "It is I who have been wronged."

"Not by me," Malak growled, his eyes narrowing in anger. "Never by me."

"Well..." She couldn't argue with that so she said the only thing she could think of. "You kissed me without permission. Just now. And you kept me from defending myself against a stupid dragon."

"Dragons happen to be very smart and very temperamental. Had you debated him, he would have eaten you to win the argument. I saved your life by kissing you. In fact, this is the second time I've come to your aid and you have yet to thank me for it. Maybe I should have let him eat you. Then I could go back to living my normal carefree life."

"Oh, I'm so sorry to get kidnapped for the second time. I didn't mean to disrupt whatever sordid thing you have going on here with my presence." She threw up her hands, trying to act nonchalant but secretly jealous of the idea of Malak with other women. "If you recall, I left willingly. It is not my fault your world keeps dragging me back."

"You've had a rough time. Why don't you go get some rest and we'll discuss this later?" Malak looked as if he were going to leave her.

"I don't need rest. I've been resting for so long I

couldn't sleep if I wanted to. What do you think Cupid had me doing for the last several days? It wasn't like we had lively conversations over mead. Every time I woke up, he'd knock me out again with his powders."

Malak looked up. "He took you from your home right away? Hmm, he must have been waiting for the red moon to deliver you to me knowing you couldn't go home until the season was over."

"So glad you have it all figured out." She lifted her hands. "Tell me, what exactly are my choices here? I'm trapped in this world for however long. My sister is off touring the magic realm with her husband and the only people I know are..."

"Are?" he prompted when she didn't finish.

"I don't want to be a burden."

"Then don't be." He said it like it was the easiest decision in the world.

"What other choice is there for me? At least back in my world I could fend for myself." She laughed in disbelief. "I know my options, Malak. Larus made them clear before I left. I can either marry a complete stranger or I can live off him and my sister. Mina has felt responsible for me all my life. I do not want to impede upon her happiness."

"Is that the real reason you went back?" Malak studied her intently. She didn't know who had stepped closer, but the distance between them had lessened. The night breeze hit her back and she shivered, rubbing her bare arms.

"One of them," she admitted.

"And the others?"

"I don't expect a man like you to understand." Sophia sighed, shaking her head.

"Try me. You might be surprised."

"No. You won't understand. You have more women than there are days in a year. You were probably down in the hall with them when Cupid brought me here." Her eyes were drawn to his lips as he spoke. She could still taste him on her tongue from when he kissed her.

"I haven't been with anyone since I first saw you."

She'd never seen him look more serious. Foolish or not, she believed him. Her heart fluttered and she couldn't breathe for a long moment. "Really?"

He nodded once. "So, try me. What is it you don't think I'll understand?"

"I loved Larus," Sophia said. Malak's brows lowered in an instant glare. Was he jealous?

"You lie." The words weren't as forceful as usual.

"No, I loved him. Deeply. And I loved Devlin just as much. You can't know what it's like to love like that and then have it taken away as if it were nothing. Devlin looked at me with his vampire eyes and I loved him.

Now, all I have is an empty memory to remind me what love can be like and the knowledge that at any time someone can come along and do it again."

"You didn't love Larus," Malak insisted. "It was a potion."

"Potion or not, it felt real to me."

"There is a way," he insisted. "A way that no enchantment of that kind can harm you again. You can stay here, with your sister, in this realm."

She thought of her childhood home. He was right. It wasn't a pleasant prospect and being a lone woman traveling to France wasn't a safe bet either. She knew that she'd been too stubborn to admit to it before now. "I know. I can end it by marrying someone. But how can I do that?"

"I saw what you had to go back to, Sophia. You would be better off here. Your sister is married to a king. That does count for something and I would offer my home to you as well. There is no need for you to starve."

"I can't accept your charity and I'm afraid of what the payment would be if I were to stay here with you." She closed her eyes. The idea of being Malak's lover did hold some appeal, but she wouldn't be able to bare the ending of their time. Or if he went to another, she'd die a little inside. "As to marriage, how can I bind someone to me for eternity knowing that whatever we feel for each other isn't nearly what it should be? I'd be using him for protection and he'd get what?" She shrugged delicately. "A wife that married him because she had no choice?"

Malak grinned. "I can think of a few rewards to such a thing."

Sophia tried, but she couldn't suppress a small laugh. What was it about this man? Did he have to be so... *appealing?*

"You could always take me up on my offer." His eyes didn't leave hers.

Sophia shivered, remembering what it was like to be in his arms. His skin was so hard and warm and when he kissed her, she felt it all the way to her toes. Drawn to him, she couldn't seem to stop herself. She was so alone and she only felt safe when in his arms. If ever she needed someone to hold her, now was the time. Lightly, she touched his cheek.

"What are you doing?" he asked, his voice hoarse.

"I'm offering myself to you, Malak. I believe you. I trust you to have told me the truth about us not being under a spell."

"I've never lied to you."

"I believe that. I do." Running her hand down his smooth chest, she trembled. Desire wound its way down her arm, filling her stomach with need. Her breasts ached for his kisses, for his touch. One time in his bed wasn't enough. She wanted to be completely aware this time. Trying to sound tough and detached, she said, "I'm going to let you... *lift my skirts*, but it doesn't mean I've changed my mind about anything, got it? I might still walk out that door after we're done. I'm doing it for me, not you. This has nothing to do with you."

"I beg to differ. This has a lot to do with me," Malak said.

"Well, if you don't want to do it, I can always ask Devlin to come get me." She started to walk away.

Malak grabbed her arm, turning her into his embrace. His words a growl, he threatened, "Don't you dare."

"One sword is as good as any other." Her words were low. Being nonchalant was harder than she thought.

As if seeing through her pretense, he laughed. "Spoken like a woman who's never been to battle."

Okay, she could admit when she'd gotten herself in over her head. She stopped moving, letting her hand rest above his heart. Unable to look him in the eye, she whispered, "Malak?"

As if sensing her need, he cupped her cheek and lifted her mouth to his. She was surprised at how tenderly his lips moved along hers. Slowly, he turned her, kissing her as he backed her up against the stone. It was a strange contrast to the warm plains of his chest. His tongue slid against the crease of her lips before thrusting past to explore every inch of her mouth. A shock or pure ecstasy went through her, stirring her blood like never before.

Sophia moaned, grabbing his face to keep him close. His hands were on her body, touching every inch of her as he deftly stripped her of her dress. The cool breeze tickled her naked flesh as she was exposed, but his looming body kept her warmer than the gown ever could. The emptiness she felt left her when she was with him, whether they were fighting or kissing, she felt safe, complete. From the first moment, she'd wanted him. But that is what scared her. How could she want someone so much without being under a spell? How could Malak's nearness make her feel so complete as if she'd found what she'd been looking for all her life?

His mouth left hers and she gasped for air. Her heart pounded as if she'd ran for miles. Malak's lips didn't stop. He drew his mouth over her neck, nipping and biting at her flesh. Sharp fangs pierced into her, but she didn't care. Let him mark her again. She knew in this perfect moment that she could never belong to any other.

Sophia was tired of fighting her feelings. Maybe things could work out. So what if the odds weren't good? That had never scared her in the past.

He slid his hands boldly over her chest to cup her breasts in his palms. Small bonfires of pleasure erupted on her nipples, sending a trail of fiery passion throughout her blood. The rough material of his clothing rubbed against her, hiding the press of his erection. She grabbed at his waist, pulling frantically at the material until it came loose. Jerking him forward, the large press of his shaft burned her with its need and she couldn't help but respond.

Then, to her surprise, his hot kisses left her nipples and moved lower. A gold fire burned within his shifted eyes, adding an exciting danger to his touch. With a low growl sounding in his throat, he kneeled before her. The breeze stung her breasts with cold where he'd wetted them.

Malak grabbed her leg and pulled it over his shoulders. Only too late did she realize what he was doing. She gasped as his mouth closed over her sex, licking like she was the sweets at the end of a banquet. His sharp fangs teased the sensitive flesh but didn't hurt her as he did delightful things with his long tongue.

His hands ran over her length, touching everywhere they could from his position between her legs. She grabbed his hair, at first because she was going to pull him back, but as he latched his mouth onto her, rolling his tongue along the sensitive bud he found hidden within her folds, she pulled him tighter against her.

She'd never felt anything so glorious. Hard fangs

combined with the soft probe of his tongue and she couldn't stop her hips from thrusting forward in acceptance. His kissed moved lower, dipping intimately inside her.

"Malak," she gasped, rocking her hips harder, riding his mouth.

He growled passionately, his fingers replacing his tongue inside her body as he stretched her. Her knees weakened and she reached behind her head to hold herself up, clutching onto the uneven stone of the wall. She cried out, riding his hand even as his mouth continued its intimate massage. It felt so good she couldn't stop.

He curled his fingers and she trembled in delight at the sensation. Malak was in her head. She felt him, magnifying her passion with his own. The pleasure mounted, pouring over as she came in one blissful moment of jerking perfection.

Malak tilted his head back and howled. Sophia collapsed into a shivering mass. Instantly, he grabbed her, lifting her into his strong arms. His steps eager, he carried her down the stairwell toward his chambers. Laying her down on the bed, he groaned as he came next to her. His hard shaft rubbed against her hip and she realized that while she'd taken pleasure, he had yet to find his release.

With a playful laugh, she rolled him onto his back.

Her body was wonderfully numb, but she quickly found strength as she tasted his flesh. Licking and biting a light trail over his chest, she licked one nipple and then the other. Malak's body strained as he squirmed beneath her touch.

"So sweet," he whispered, his voice gruff in his native tongue.

His hand rubbed her shoulders, pushing her insistently lower with each kiss until she was close to his navel. Rimming the small hole, she heard him gasp. His hands pushed, urging her to go down.

"Is this what you want?" she asked, licking a muscular hip. Her cheek bumped the side of his arousal.

"Aye," he groaned. Grabbing her head, he pulled her mouth to his erection. "But here."

There was no modesty in him when it came to these things and Sophia found she had none as well. Everything she did seemed to bring him pleasure and he had no problem guiding her as he taught her how to fulfill their desires. His passion had fueled hers to burning. Only when he was straining and grunting did he pull her mouth off his arousal.

"Sit on top of me," he ordered, pulling at her arms to get her to obey. She did, mindlessly yielding to his expertise in this matter. Her sex rubbed along his hard stomach and she wiggled on top of him, stimulating herself against him.

"Mm," she moaned. Short dark hairs sprouted on his chest and she ran her fingers over them. She liked it when the beast threatened to emerge. It reminded her of all he was capable of, his strength, his power, his wild ways. The hairs spread over his stomach and she moaned as the friction of them tickled her sex. Rocking harder on his stomach, she groaned, "I love your skin."

"You torture the beast," he growled. "Take me now. Lift before I lose all control."

Malak grabbed her breasts, pinching her nipples. There was something to his smell, his untamed look that took away every doubt, every sense of pain or fear. Grabbing her hips, he pushed her back so that she was seated next to his erection. The shaft seemed larger than before but she couldn't see it to confirm. Golden eyes stared at her and she felt a sense of power as she wiggled her butt along his shaft.

"Sophia," he groaned, pleading with her to end her torment. "You don't know what you're doing. I... *argh*."

Fascinated, she watched his face. Something inside her drove her on. "Does the wolf want to come out and play?" She lifted herself, reaching between them to draw the tip of his shaft along her opening. "Is this what the big, bad beast wants?"

Looking down between her thighs, she stiffened. It wasn't her imagination. He had grown in size. The tip of his thick shaft dipped along her moist folds, parting her lips as he aligned his body. Malak grabbed her hips and pulled. Claws dug into her flesh as his hands slid onto her upper thighs. He was too strong and he didn't stop as he impaled her, stretching her.

Malak roared. It was a victorious sound. The fullness of him didn't rip her apart as she feared it would, but instead filled her with a burning need. Digging her nails into his chest, she squirmed with him deep inside, wiggling back and forth.

His hands kneaded her thighs and he looked to be in pain. "You're so small, so fragile."

Leaning forward, she lifted her hips and whispered, "I'm not going to break so easily, my lord wolf."

Malak moaned and she sat back on his lap. The movement felt amazing and she did it again, lifting and falling against him. The tension built anew, mind-numbing in its intensity. Like an animal she took over, riding him hard, ramming his body into hers. There was no pain, not like the first time, only pure realm-shattering pleasure as they climaxed in unison.

Sophia fell against his chest, unable to move and not wanting to. What a strange, long adventure it had been, getting to this moment. Whatever the future brought, she would not regret being with Malak.

"I'm sorry," he whispered, not stirring beneath her, except for the heavy rise and fall of his chest.

She frowned. Okay, well, at least *she* didn't have any regrets. "There is nothing to be sorry for. You didn't hurt me."

"I know, but..."

"You're not going to apologize for taking advantage of me, are you? Because that would ruin the moment. I'm a big girl, Malak, and I make my choices. I choose to be with you."

He laughed softly. "I don't know any other mortal woman who would admit to that so easily. Most of you hide from your passion."

She lifted, moving to dance her fingers along his chest. "Do I look like I'm hiding?"

"I'm sorry because I didn't ask permission." He looked serious.

"If you noticed, I didn't stop to ask you if you minded being bedded either, so I think we're even."

"Mm, no, not for that. I didn't ask permission before..." He paused. "Let me ask you something first. Would you mate to me, Sophia? If I asked you to, would you mate to me with the knowledge that I know what you said earlier and I accept the fact that you don't love me as you thought to have loved others?" His eyes fell and she felt as if his pain was her own. It tore at her insides. "Would you stay here, with me, as my mate?"

"Are you asking?" she breathed, her body unable to move. Inside her mind screamed, 'Yes. Yes. A thousand times yes.'

'Was that a yes?'

Sophia tensed. Malak's voice was in her head. 'How...?'

'It's the mind link. It's how the other lycans and I communicate with each other in lycan form and it's how mates communicate after they've...'

"Did you say mates?" Sophia gasped. Pleasure ran through her at his confession. "We're...? You and I?"

He nodded. "I couldn't stop myself. You were so beautiful cast in red moonlight and you tasted so sweet and I looked up at you and suddenly, it happened. You were in my head as well as my heart."

He looked as if he expected her to yell at him for binding her against her will. Slowly, she smiled. "I'm glad you did it."

"What? You're not mad? I know how you value your independence—"

She shushed him by placing her hand to his lips. "I'm happy you did it because it proves that you love me as much as I've loved you from the very beginning. I saw you and I felt so much more than I ever did for Devlin and Larus combined. That's what scared me. I was frightened that it wasn't real. But knowing you couldn't control yourself, knowing you had to have me, as I burned to have you..." She smiled, her love shining from her eyes as she looked at him. "When I stepped through that portal and you didn't stop me..."

"I couldn't. I gave my word to see you through it."

"I know and I was too stubborn to stop from leaving. But the moment I landed in the mortal realm I knew I'd made a mistake. I was scared. I just thought if I could go to where it all began, I could fix myself. Can you forgive me for being scared?"

"There is nothing to forgive." Malak growled, grabbing her and flipping her on her back. He devoured her neck with kisses, repeating over and over, "I love you, Sophia, I love you. You are mine."

Cupid gulped as he looked at the three very angry lycans and their even more repulsive lovesick mates. Lady Sophia, the supposed tool of Malak's hate, reeked of her husband's scent. And, to make matters worse, her belly was swollen with the lycan's child, and Lady Mina was almost as round. Cupid shivered in disgust. The women were all rosy-cheeked and bright eyed. They looked happy and that made him miserable. Hearing a baby cry, he grimaced. He'd forgotten Lady Rhiannon had given birth only a week before. The sound of the child tore at him and he clawed his head, trying to dig his wrinkled, gnarled fingers into his ears.

"Ach. Bah." Cupid cried. "Enough."

"Say it's over, Cupid," Sophia demanded, her voice like twinkling stars.

"Swear by every wart on your body," Rhiannon added.

"Or we promise to name every single baby we have after his sweet cherub of an Uncle Cupid." Mina grinned.

Cupid screamed, a high-pitched sound of horror. "I promise. I promise. I will no longer meddle in your lives."

"And the lives of others," Larus said.

"Aye, aye, only don't call me their uncle. That hideous, horrible pink-cheeked bundle of..." Cupid gagged, tearing his eyes away from Rhiannon and Ilar's baby. "I promise not to meddle in the lives of lycans again. Just get the baby away from me."

"Good," Ilar said.

"We better make him swear it," Malak added.

"I swear it," Cupid howled. "Now please, get that baby out of here and take the round ones with you." He motioned at the pregnant women, before moaning, "Ruined. I'm ruined. Three lovers. Ruined."

"I think he gets the point," Sophia said.

"Hmm, aye, I don't think he'll be meddling in our lives anymore." Malak wrapped his arm around his mate and grinned, kissing her temple. Cupid gagged, closing his eyes tight.

"If we find you've lied to us today, we'll make sure everyone know what you did," Larus warned.

"They already know," Cupid wailed, thinking of the baskets of love darts that filled his cave. He was running out of places to get rid of the offensive things. Already he'd darted all his goats with them, making them fall in love with trees. What other use was there for such magic?

"He means the mortal world as well," Sophia said, laughing. "We'll make a day each year honoring your trade as a creature of love. The whole world, for all eternity, will think of Cupid when they think of love."

Cupid screeched, beating his feet on the ground.

"I think we've tortured him enough," Rhiannon laughed. "Come on, Ilar. Let's get your son home."

Cupid kept his eyes closed until they'd walked away. Standing, he patted the dirt into his clothes, trying to make the filth stay. Then, turning, he laughed. "Stupid lycans. Stupid lycan mates. I promised not to meddle in the lives of lycans and those three couples. I said nothing about the lives of mortals, or of their half human, half lycan children."

Tossing his head back, he laughed heartily. Let them think they've won for now, at least until they named their children.

"Foolish, foolish lycans. Don't they know there isn't a creature alive who can best a clever troll?"

The End

Come say hello! Michelle loves talking with readers on social media!

www.MichellePillow.com

facebook.com/AuthorMichellePillow

twitter.com/michellepillow

instagram.com/michellempillow

bookbub.com/authors/michelle-m-pillow

goodreads.com/Michelle_Pillow

amazon.com/author/michellepillow

youtube.com/michellepillow

pinterest.com/michellepillow

COMPLIMENTARY EXCERPT

TRY BEFORE YOU BUY!

King of the Unblessed

Urban Fantasy Romance
Realm Immortal Book One

Merrick, King of the Unblessed, was once heir to all that is good—happiness and pleasure his domain. Now, trapped as the ruler of mischief, he stands on a precipice of choice. On one side his estranged brother, now ruler of what should have been Merrick's, and on the other King Lucien of the Damned. Both would sway him. Damnation is winning.

Lady Juliana of Bellemare is protected by the Blessed, targeted by the Damned and, now, coveted by the Unblessed. Betrothed to an old friend of her father's, Juliana is resigned to living out her days close to her childhood home. She longs for an adventure, never dreaming she'll get what she wishes for when her fiancé is murdered and the children of Bellemare are stolen. To set things right, Juliana embarks on a quest through a strange realm where nothing is as it seems.

Merrick brings more adventure and passion than any woman could want. Can she withstand the temptations of the Unblessed King? Desperate to be the one to rule her and unaccustomed to taking no for an answer, Merrick offers her a choice: come with him until he tires of her...or die.

Chapter One Excerpt

Black Palace of the Unblessed, Kingdom of Valdis, 1406 AD

Immortality had a way of changing fate. None knew this as well as Merrick, dark elfin King of Valdis, ruler of all that was unblessed. Once, long ago in a time he did not like to remember, he'd been heir to the Tegwen throne, future King of the Blessed. Happiness and pleasure had been his, as had love—love of a family, of his people. He'd been light and good. Now he was ruler of all that was dark and feared.

Well, not all that was dark. King Lucien of the Damned did have rule over the demons.

As Merrick gazed upon the narrow basin of water before him, the liquid was still. It reflected his eyes—eyes so brown they looked to be black. When he was angry, the whites would fill in with the dark color. Those who saw the change often claimed to see the demon lurking beneath his surface. His eyes were a strange contrast to his long blond hair. They were a reflection of what he'd become, changed the day of his Unblessed Coronation. The hair was a reminder of what he'd once been.

The divining basin was perched atop a tall column, which in turn was lifted up on a platform in the center of the dark garden. It had been a gift from King Lucien upon Merrick's coronation. His powers were somewhat connected to the Demon King, even though his coronation had been the first and last time he'd spoken directly with the man. The gray stone base was carved with images of demons sucking the souls from mortals. Within the shallow pool, the moonlight reflected on water to reveal to him all he would see, always the present, but sometimes the future and past. King Merrick didn't look to the future, for the images were blurred and often misread, and he refused to dwell on the past.

Silver moonlight shone over the expansive black garden. The plants were withered and neglected, yet did not die. Dark stone paths led up from his castle palace, twisting about the grounds in a seemingly endless pattern. They were surrounded by thick walls covered in vines. The walls formed a labyrinth from which trespassers could never escape. Thorns, as sharp as blades, edged the vines. Amongst the thorns, crimson flowers blossomed, but they only did so for him. The flowers looked almost liquid, as if the petals would drip like blood to the ground. They were the only flowers in the immortal realm that would bloom when he was near.

Repeatedly, Merrick watched his presence suck the life from the world around him. He was necessary, as necessary as light and spring. He was fall, winter, death to the land. Without him, the immortal world would not rest. Without him, good would not be. And for this he was hated by those he'd once called friends.

"Show me that which I seek," Merrick ordered the water softly. He tapped a finger against the surface, rippling it. He knew what was to come. It tortured him as it soothed him. It filled him with longing and frustration. From the frustration came anger, and from the anger a bitterness he didn't try to hide.

Then there she was, sitting and staring at a fire, a look of longing in her eyes. He later discovered she did that often. The human woman had captured his notice one night as he flew around the mortal realm masquerading as a falcon. Unless magick favored it, which wasn't often, the falcon disguise was the only way he could go to the mortal realm in solid form for long periods of time. Otherwise he could only project a glamour of himself or send his minions in his place.

Merrick hadn't thought, had just watched her like he would a play. He loved her, or at least thought he could love her, as much as any being with a dark heart could love. Love was not so lofty an emotion and was wrongly thought exclusive to the blessed. However, as with all things, the emotion was more complicated than that, for love could be as dark as the underworld, as enslaving as death, as vengeful as a righteous cause. Beings killed in the name of love, died for it, lusted after it, greedily kept it locked away, withheld it, exploited it. This was not an emotion the King of the Unblessed sought to possess.

"I, Lady Juliana of Bellemare," she'd said that first evening he saw her, "have come here to slay your village dragon in return for my weight in gold."

Her voice had been low and soft, like a lullaby, but such voices he'd heard many times before her. Nymphs had been brought to his castle to sing and they were renowned for the sounds they made. Right away, he knew she spoke only to herself, imagining a world beyond that with which she was acquainted. Dragons didn't exist in her world. Then again, he didn't exist in her world. Immortals preferred to keep the humans unaware, for they were uninteresting creatures who lacked power and magic. Mortals were ruled by fear and ignorance and King Merrick was amused to watch where that ignorance would lead them. But Lady Juliana was different than other mortal women, for she'd captured his notice. That alone marked her as special.

Why it should be so, he didn't understand. She was beautiful, with long dark hair and wide blue eyes, but Merrick had seen too much of beauty to be swayed easily by it. For if beauty could conquer him, then just the sight of the Golden Palace at Tegwen would have done him in long ago.

No, there was no reason for it. All he knew was that night after night he was drawn to the garden basin to watch her. At first he'd hoped to find fault with her, thus losing interest. But the more he watched, the more he longed for her, wanted her, until she entered his thoughts when he was away from the garden.

Merrick knew obsession only led to madness. The creatures of Valdis wouldn't be pleased with an obsessed king, not when they struggled constantly with Tegwen, and with each other. There were many who wanted his throne. Only death would relinquish him of it and no matter how he tired of life, he didn't wish for death.

The water rippled over the vision. Juliana stood, stretching her arms above her head. Though fine by human standards, her russet gown was woolen and plain.

The long trailing sleeves touched the floor, sweeping up over her elbows. The bodice was high and the skirts hung loose, hiding her figure beneath the padded underskirts. She didn't cover her dark locks, but let them hang freely to her waist.

Merrick frowned. There was only one option left to him. He'd go to her and offer her a choice. Either she would come with him until he tired of her or he would have her killed. If he possessed her, had her locked away in his castle, then he wouldn't be so obsessed. Lady Juliana would be under his complete control. If she chose death, then he'd no longer be able to gaze upon her face, unless it was to see it rotting in the ground. The spell would be broken and he would be free of her.

Merrick watched her for a moment longer, then waved his hand over the basin. Her image disappeared. He stared at the water a moment longer, contemplating his decision. It was for the best. He did not like the distraction she caused him.

Soon. He would offer his bargain to her soon. Death or enslavement. Balling his hand into a fist, Merrick really hoped she chose death.

To find out more about Michelle's books visit www.MichellePillow.com

www.ingramcontent.com/pod-product-compliance
Lightning Source LLC
Chambersburg PA
CBHW050144110726
47898CB00008B/2660